Goodbye, Mr Hitler

Jackie French

Angus&Robertson
An imprint of HarperCollins*Children'sBooks*, Australia

First published in Australia in 2017
by HarperCollins*Publishers* Australia Pty Limited
ABN 36 009 913 517
harpercollins.com.au

HarperCollins*Publishers*
Level 13, 201 Elizabeth Street, Sydney NSW 2000, Australia
Unit D1, 63 Apollo Drive, Rosedale, Auckland 0632, New Zealand
A 53, Sector 57, Noida, UP, India
1 London Bridge Street, London SE1 9GF, United Kingdom
2 Bloor Street East, 20th floor, Toronto, Ontario M4W 1A8, Canada
195 Broadway, New York NY 10007, USA

National Library of Australia Cataloguing-in-Publication data:

French, Jackie, author.
Goodbye, Mr Hitler / Jackie French.
ISBN: 978 1 4607 5129 9 (paperback)
ISBN: 978 1 4607 0594 0 (ebook)
For children.
Hitler, Adolf, 1889–1945 — Juvenile fiction.
World War, 1939–1945 — Germany — Juvenile fiction.
Refugee children — Australia — Juvenile fiction.

Cover design by Hazel Lam, HarperCollins Design Studio
Cover images: Boy by Nicola Smith / Trevillion Images; (from left to right) Migrant
Arrivals in Australia, NAA: A12111, 1/1954/4/53; Fairsea by Graeme Andrews
Collection — Sydney Heritage Fleet; paper texture by shutterstock.com
Author photograph by Kelly Sturgiss
Typeset in Sabon by Kelli Lonergan.

Printed and bound by CPI Group (UK) Ltd, Croydon, CR0 4YY

To Olga Horak,
who turns evil into good

Prologue

My name is Johannes.

This is the story of how an ogre swallowed me when I was ten years old.

The ogre swallowed Frau Marks too, and Helga.

Other stories will tell you how the ogre ate forty-four million people, chewed them up and so they died.

But I do not know forty-four million people. This is the story of the three of us.

This is the story of how we three learned to live.

Chapter 1

JOHANNES
POLAND, 1943

On the corner by the park lived a house of love and stories.

A cat called Maus lived in the house too. Maus was supposed to eat the mice she was named for. Instead she sat on any book Opa was reading at his desk and purred.

The bookcase climbed up two whole walls. Johannes's stories were on the lower shelves, bright volumes about a cow who thought she was a dog and sat on the lap of the farmer's wife, as Johannes sat on Opa's lap and listened to him reading. Opa read him the books over and over, for as long as Johannes yelled, 'More!'

There was only one book on Johannes's shelves that he'd asked Opa never to read again. The book had bright flowers in a forest on the cover and a smiling boy, so you did not know till you were halfway through the book that an ogre lived inside. The ogre ate small children until one day he ate a clever boy who tricked him by tickling his stomach. The ogre burped and all the children were saved. Even though it had a happy ending, Johannes did not

3

want to hear the story again. It was not worth being frightened for half a book, just for a page of happy ending.

The top shelves had books no one was allowed to read. Books hidden behind other books, secret books: books that could bring trouble if anyone knew that they were there.

One day, soon after, Opa became ill. He moved away the books at the front of the top shelves and showed Johannes books from towards the back.

'Here is Thomas Mann, and his brother, Heinrich Mann, and Heinrich Heine,' said Opa softly, his old hands stroking the leather covers. 'These are the great thinkers of the world. We now live in a country that burns men like these, that burns their words and their thoughts. But words kept in the heart cannot be burned. Remember the books are here. And one day, when no one burns books any more, these words will be yours too.'

'Yes, Opa,' said Johannes. But the books were big and he was small and they had no clever cows on the front cover, in fact no pictures in them at all, or anything but words. He could not see why books like that could be important.

Opa died that year, of the grippe. Even though Johannes's father was an important doctor, with his own small hospital, even though Mutti had been a doctor too before she married, and still helped sometimes at the hospital, they could not save Opa.

Opa held Johannes's hand before he closed his eyes. 'Words in the heart,' he whispered.

'Words in the heart,' repeated Johannes, and he saw Opa smile. He was not sure what that meant, but he was glad Opa smiled at the end.

Chapter 2

On Tuesday Frau Marks took food down to the two jüdische children hidden behind the false wall in the coal cellar of the Sisters of Compassion Maternity Hospital.

Forty-three children had passed through the cellar at some time: lost children, orphaned children, their parents sent to concentration camps, sometimes to work, but mostly just to die.

Sometimes, as the desperate procession of jüdische families trudged through the streets, hoping against the evidence that there might be life beyond the trains waiting like crocodiles on the tracks, a baby might quickly be passed to a sympathetic woman standing in the street who held out her arms in a sudden rush of courage and compassion.

'Even in times like these,' said Sister Columba, 'there are those who cheer the Führer with their mouths, but mercy still sings inside their hearts.'

Sometimes those who saw a baby being saved in this manner did not call to the Gestapo, 'Here! Arrest this traitor and the jüdische Kindchen.'

Other times one of the Sisters walked a little way with the marchers to pray with them, for although Hitler condemned all who had any jüdisches blood, some were Christian too. The Sister could hide a baby in her robes, then step back into the crowd. Sometimes, when a family was rounded up, a neighbour or friend might keep a small child back, pretending it was theirs, hurrying it away so it did not cry out for its parents.

And when members of the congregation saved such a child they might go to the priest for help; and Father Reinhardt would have the child taken to the hospital to be hidden by the Sisters for a while.

Only forty-three children, from all the millions who had marched towards the death camps. 'We cannot save millions,' said Sister Columba. 'But every child we rescue is a miracle.'

'Do not waste your life weeping over what we cannot do,' Sister Columba had told Frau Marks when she first came back to work at the hospital. 'Do not waste your life on hate. We must keep our strength to save the few we can. Each time we save a child, feel joy lift up your heart at what you can do, instead of sinking beneath the weight of what you can't.'

It was best not to know the children's names. Best that the children forgot too. For children could not hide in a coal cellar for months or years. Children's bodies as well as spirits needed sunlight. One by one they vanished, delivered secretly to families who would hide them by saying that the child was their dead sister's, orphaned by the bombing. These days there were many orphans. No one looked too closely at children, not when the sky rained bombs, when whole villages crumbled into matchsticks, when in a second the world around you might turn to fire and rubble. Most children were wide-eyed and starved now. If these children screamed in terror in the night, so did many others as the planes wept bombs each night.

One day the war might end. One day these two children might remember that once they had names that weren't Pieter and Gretchen, might be reunited with mothers, fathers, grandmothers, and learn once again who they had been born to be.

But for now 'Pieter' and 'Gretchen' huddled mouse-like in the small brick room, with a single candle for their light. Father Reinhardt brought extra candles when he came to say Mass each Sunday. In wartime there were many who lit a candle for their loved ones, and if that candle burned to keep the darkness from huddled children, 'It did good twice,' said Father Reinhardt.

Today Frau Marks wore her nurse's uniform as she carried the tray down to the cellar. The tray held two chamberpots covered with a linen cloth. One held water and one held bread and jam, although the jam was mostly turnip and the bread was bran and bark. But that was all the nurses and the Sisters had to share these days, with cabbage or turnip soup, and sometimes a potato. You ate, you lived. In this sixth year of war, that was enough.

Most patients brought their own food to the maternity hospital: rich chicken broth in Thermoses, white bread and even cakes. These days the only women sent to hospital to have their babies were the wives of Nazi officers, the few people in Germany who ate well. Sometimes there were scraps from the patients' meals to give the children, but not today.

Frau Marks checked no one was watching before she opened the cellar door. A maternity hospital was a good place to hide children — few patients stayed more than a fortnight; nor did they wander far from their babies and their beds. Additionally,

7

the Sisters insisted on regular visiting hours, though even Sister Columba could not refuse a high-ranking Nazi officer who wanted to see his baby son.

The corridor was clear. Sister Columba and Sister Martin would patrol on either side too. That was another reason the maternity hospital was a good place to hide children. One nun in a white habit was easily mistaken for another. A nun could vanish for a day and a night, and say they had been praying if a patient missed them.

The Sisters of Compassion Maternity Hospital was a good place to hide a woman too. Frau Marks had hidden there for five years, since the students killed her husband, screaming, 'Jude!' as they pushed him from a second-storey window till he lay broken on the paving stones below.

He had not been jüdisch. Oh, his grandmother had been, perhaps. But not her Simon. Simon had been a poet, a professor, an Englishman in love with German literature and with her. They and their son were happy in their house with flowered sofas and fat cushions and feather-stuffed quilts aired in the sun.

Smashed. Cut from her in one outburst of horror. And in those frantic seconds she could not even cradle his body. All she could do for Simon now was save their son.

She had run, holding Georg by the hand. Georg at ten years old loved the Führer, loved his country, loved his parents too. But suddenly Georg was jüdisch. The Nazis killed his father, and they would come for him.

Her sister, Gudrun, let them stay in her home for three hours. No more, not for a sister who had shamed her by marrying a jüdisch man.

Three hours to phone Maria, who had tried to tell her, tried to warn her. Maria, who knew a friend who knew a friend. And at the end of that three hours Georg was gone. Had he reached

8

England and safety, as she hoped? To his Aunt Miriam? Bombs fell on England now — would he be safe even there?

She had asked Gudrun to forward any letters to her to a shop Maria had suggested, a safe place where they might be collected. No word had come. Or perhaps it had, but Gudrun had destroyed the letters.

Gudrun had spat 'Jude' as if, by marrying Simon, Frau Marks had contaminated their family. By Hitler's rules, of course, she had. Their friends at the university had not moved to save their colleague as the students wrestled him across the hall and out the window.

No safety with Simon's colleagues or her family. They had disowned her now.

She had waited a night and day to make sure Georg was out of Germany, in case they captured her and made her talk, at a railway station waiting room that night, then lingering in cafés, pretending to drink coffee, all the next day. As it grew dark, she slipped into their old house one final time without turning on the lights, gathering money, jewellery, her passports, British and German, her nursing certificate, the deeds to the house, all in one small suitcase, praying no one had reported her to the Gestapo yet, that Simon's death had not yet triggered a hunt for his family.

She took a train, a bus, a train, showing her German passport, the one in her maiden name, the name on her nursing certificate, criss-crossing the country in case anyone might try to trace her. And then she walked.

And came here, to the hospital where she had worked before her marriage. She had told the Sisters everything, so they knew they would risk their lives to shelter her.

Sister Columba had smiled. Sister Columba, who had rapped her hard over the knuckles each time she made a mistake as a nursing student, and made her scrub the chamberpots. 'We know what Christ would do,' said Sister Columba calmly now.

Frau Marks became Nurse Stöhlich. The new papers said that was her name. She had stayed in the tiny attic room until Sister Columba gave her the forgeries, and the roster for her to work. Good work: helping babies into the world. She had to keep believing it was good work, even if they were Nazi babies who might one day work for Herr Hitler, the man who had stolen her life.

Had stolen so many millions more.

Frau Marks did not know when the Sisters had begun to hide jüdische children. She thought it was a year, perhaps, before they asked her to help too. Being wanted by the Gestapo did not make you trustworthy. It was easy to sell information to the Gestapo to save yourself, but the Sisters trusted her now. Trusted her not to walk to a Gestapo office and say, 'I will show you a whole network of resistance workers, hiding Juden, if you will let me go free to neutral Switzerland, where I might begin the journey to find my son.'

And so tonight Frau Marks clicked on the light and walked down the stairs to the coal cellar. A hospital for Nazi women had electric lights. She opened the hidden door and saw the second of terror on the children's faces. Pieter was two years old, perhaps, his sister four. Old enough to know they were not safe, if the wrong person found them.

Sister Columba lifted the two children from her lap and stood up stiffly. Even though she had walked through the coal cellar, her robe was not dusty. Frau Marks had practised that too.

'All well?' asked Sister Columba.

Frau Marks forced herself to smile. She might only be able to bring the children bread and jam and water, but she could smile. Georg, she thought, looking at Pieter, remembering Georg when he had been two years old too. Georg had blond hair as these children now had, bleached to help disguise them. One day, perhaps, the children might let their hair grow dark again.

One day, the war would end.

'Frau Weber has had a baby girl: six pounds, two ounces. She is doing well. Frau Sternberg and Frau von Hüber have arrived.'

Sister Columba nodded. She would melt back into the hospital's two wards and six private rooms as if she had never left. She took Frau Marks's hands in her own, old and papery and strong, and held them in a brief silent prayer.

And then she shut the door behind her.

Frau Marks kept her smile. 'Who would like a story?'

Gretchen nodded. Pieter said nothing, clutching Gretchen's hand.

Frau Marks put down the tray, then sat on the pile of sacks, still warm from Sister Columba's body, and took the children on her lap. Touch was important. They could give these children so little apart from food and sanctuary, except touch and love and human warmth.

She handed them the bread, the jam, all at once. They had given up trying to make hungry children eke food out over a day and night, and it was too risky to visit the cellar more than once every twenty-four hours. Better they eat just once a day.

Georg, she thought again. But Georg had been a laughing baby. These children hardly moved or spoke, as if sleep was the only safety that they knew, spending hours gazing at nothing with dark eyes. But stories brought them back again, for a little while. Stories and hugs.

'Once upon a time,' said Frau Marks, feeling the beloved bones in her arms, the gentle squash of children leaning into her for warmth, both hers and theirs, 'there was a butterfly, the biggest butterfly in all the world …'

'How big?' whispered Gretchen, just as Georg had once asked, 'How big, Mutti? How big was the butterfly?'

'Big as a train! He was a train butterfly, who carried children through the clouds …'

'We cannot give our children safety,' Sister Columba had said a year earlier. 'We cannot give them laughter, for they must be quiet. We cannot properly feed their starved bodies. But we can give them joy.'

Upstairs mothers in labour were told to meditate on the blessed suffering of the saints to help them through the pain until their babies were born. Here in the darkness with the single candle, they gave the children butterflies.

Story after story, till it seemed the darkness lifted off the cellar and the world, just a little, till the candle flickered and it was time to light a new one, and to settle Gretchen and Pieter to sleep once more, their heads on Frau Marks's lap, as she stroked their smooth young foreheads and remembered Georg, as she loved them, as she loved her son …

And, at last, Frau Marks slept too.

Chapter 3

It was sad without Opa. But life had joy too. Mutti cried the first time she made cherry strudel after Opa's death. Opa had loved cherry, but it was good to remember Opa as they ate the strudel too. Vati showed Johannes how to make angel wings in the snow bank outside the house. Vati read the stories now before Johannes went to bed and sometimes, when it was grey outside, Mutti read him stories too. Opa's loss was a small ache, but his memory still made Johannes smile.

A year after Opa's death the soldier was billeted in their house.

The soldier was billeted because the house lived in a country called 'war'. War kept changing, in ways too complicated for Johannes to understand. First Germany was an enemy and then it became their leader, a country of culture and courage that would lead the world. The house and the people who lived within it had to change as the country called war changed too. The country of war meant that some boys' fathers or brothers left the village;

that 'Hello' became 'Heil Hitler'. But when your world was home, and school, and the big park of Vati's hospital, it did not matter much what the country around you was called.

At school a big new photo of Herr Hitler hung in every room now, and in the hall of Vati's hospital as well. Herr Hitler looked courageous and determined. But he looked cuddly too, quite small and with a little moustache, like someone had shaved a teddy bear. A new teacher taught them all about Herr Hitler's victories.

One day the whole world would be united under the glorious Third Reich! There would be peace and justice for all, and the world would be cleansed of Untermenschen, people who were not fit to live in the great Third Reich. Even now, Hitler's planes were conquering England, just as they had conquered Belgium, France and all the other countries marked with swastika pins on the big map of the world in the classroom.

Herr Hitler's victory stories were so exciting that it was easy to ignore the tears of boys whose brothers had been wounded or had died, and anyway, the Führer, who was Hitler, would never cry. Crying was for girls.

And Johannes knew Vati would never have to go to war. Vati's hospital was too important, a sanatorium for those who had tuberculosis. Important Nazi Party members were patients there.

The soldier billeted in their house was a major, an important man, because their house was the best one in the village. The major had a room with a good fire, and Lottie fed him on produce from the hospital's orchards and vegetable gardens, hens and pigs.

The major was a tall thin man, with a nose like an eagle's beak and tired eyes. Johannes hoped he would tell him exciting Hitler stories too. But the major stayed in his room when he came home each day, and Lottie took his meals to him there.

The major stayed there for every meal until the night dinner was late because Lottie and Mutti had been working at the hospital. Johannes had eaten bread and cheese to stop his tummy rumbling as he did his homework. But at last the good smell of chicken stew came from the kitchen — Lottie and Mutti must be back. He left his books and walked down to the living room, but turned as he heard a step behind him.

The major!

Johannes bowed politely. 'Guten Tag, Herr Major!' He pronounced the German proudly, glad that his accent was good.

The major ignored Johannes. He brushed past into the living room.

Mutti must have heard his steps too. She came quickly from the kitchen, taking off her apron. 'Major! I hope you have had a good day. Sit, please, I will bring coffee …'

It was not real coffee these days, but as Johannes was too young to drink coffee, according to Mutti and Vati, he didn't care.

'No coffee,' said the major. He blinked, then added, 'Danke.' He held up a bottle of vodka.

'I will get a glass,' said Mutti hurriedly. 'Johannes …' She broke off as the major put the bottle of vodka on the table and began to talk. 'Go to your room,' said Mutti softly to Johannes, but the major shook his head.

'The boy should stay! He has to know. Everybody has to know!' The major's words slurred, like they had been dragged out from the snow. His eyes did not see Mutti, or Johannes, or even the fire snickering up the chimney.

Johannes sat, trying not to hear. For the major spoke of marching down streets where the dead hung from the lamp posts, and others were piled higher than the snowdrifts; of trains with compartments that could kill everyone inside with gas; of camps where Untermenschen, Juden and many others who were unfit to live in the Third Reich were killed in tens of thousands; of letters from his family complaining that other officers sent back jewels and paintings. Why did they get none?

The vodka bottle was empty. When Mutti motioned Johannes to leave the room, the major didn't notice his departure.

The next morning the major was gone, posted to the place called 'the front line', at the edge of the country called war.

'The poor man was drunk. Homesick,' said Mutti. 'Germany is a great country. A man like your father would have heard if things were bad.' Some boys at school had whispered that their parents did not like Poland being under German command. But Mutti and Vati were more interested in medicine and the hospital and their family than in politics. They had always spoken German at home, as well as Polish, even before the country of war.

'I will ask Vati tonight,' said Johannes, sure that Vati would say the major had been sick a little in the head, for Vati had explained how sometimes things like that could happen. And Johannes smiled, for his was a house of happiness and smiles, and next month a branch of the Hitler Youth would be started in the village, and he could march and go on camps.

Vati would explain it all. And life would be sensible again.

Chapter 4

FRAU MARKS
GERMANY, NOVEMBER 1944

They came at night.

The scream woke her as she dozed against the wall as the children slept, their heads on her lap, their small bodies so warm and precious. Frau Marks froze, and then relaxed. Women in labour screamed, and then there was a baby, and smiles instead.

Babies were joy. When she had first come to the Sisters after losing Simon and Georg, she had felt no joy, not even at the gurgle of a baby, not in prayer, not in the music that had made her soul dance before. Sister Columba had saved her heart as surely as she had saved her body. One night, as they sat with Frau Hechner dozing, the contractions easing, Sister Columba asked, 'Would you undo it all, if you could? Not marry, not have your son? Avoid the pain?'

'Of course not.'

'I didn't think so. Love has two faces, always. Don't think because I am cloistered here I do not know these things. We always pay for love.'

'So I am paying?'

'More than you should, I know. But perhaps the gift of love was great as well?'

Frau Marks whispered, 'They killed my husband! I have lost my son …'

'Then look at the pain and hold it gently,' said Sister Columba. 'Hold your Simon and your Georg in your hands and see the love as well as pain. But hold it high, so you can see the joy around you too.'

'There is no joy.'

'No joy in God's great sunsets? No joy in a baby's breath? No joy at a lark's song or its dance upon the light? All these are God's gifts. If you turn your back on them, you turn your back on Him.'

'All I feel is hate,' confessed Frau Marks.

Sister Columba nodded. 'Hate is like bacteria. Hate grows inside a person and then it spreads to others, until even whole countries are infected. There is only one medicine to cure it.'

'What is that?'

'Goodness,' said Sister Columba. 'Doing good is contagious too. We must believe that. Do good things and, slowly, others will do them too, until once again the hate is driven back. But unless one person has the strength to say, "I am made of love, not hate," the world's cure cannot begin. Who do you wish to be? A woman of hate or love?'

'I … I don't know if I have the strength …'

'Not even for your son? Of course you have the strength,' said Sister Columba, then turned to their patient again as she woke with a gasp.

Tonight other women lie above us and the miracle of life continues, thought Frau Marks, resting her head back against the wall to sleep again. Babies, and the joy of new life …

Another scream from the corridor above the coal cellar. A shriek cut off sharply. And then boots tramping in the cellar beyond the hidden door.

Soldiers! Someone, one of the Nazi mothers, must have seen more than she should, had guessed, somehow. Perhaps even one of the families they had given a child to —

And then she thought no more, for the door swung open. Light glared in, so sharp it cut her eyes, so she only dimly saw the shape of the two men.

'Found them!'

She wrapped her arms around the children. Stupid. Ineffective. Instinct only: the instinct of a mother, a woman, a human being.

One of the man shadows tore her arms away. She shrieked as someone wailed on the floor above her, begged, 'No, no, no, no ...' and suddenly, far worse, silence.

Gretchen clasped Pieter in her arms, a small parcel of two children become one. And that was how the soldier killed them, bayoneting first one and then the other, in the stomach and then the throat, so they died with an anguished gurgle, Frau Marks lunging to get to them, held back by the other soldier's arms, crying, pleading ...

'No,' she gasped. '*No!*' Though it was done — the children dead — every human decency dead to kill babies like that.

'Jüdische rats,' said the soldier, wiping his bayonet on her skirts. He laughed at her expression. 'You think we should waste poison gas on them? Or bullets? Or gasoline to burn them in a pit? We save those for the enemy these days.'

She could not look again at the tiny crumpled bodies. Her mind tried to shut down, to turn all sight to night. She could not walk. The soldier with the bayonet dragged her by the arm, the hair, across the cellar to the stairs. She managed to stumble up them. In the hall an old woman stared at her. A stranger in a white nightdress, streaked with blood, a white cap, bloody as well.

The stranger gazed at her with Sister Columba's eyes. Eyes that looked at her, at the body of Sister Martin curled up in death upon the floor, looked at them both with love, not at the soldiers in the corridor with hate.

'Macht schnell,' said the officer. 'Hurry.'

Frau Marks managed to whisper, 'Where are we going?'

'You are going to work. To have the chance to serve the Fatherland as nurses, which is more than you deserve, traitorous cows. Far more.'

We have served the Fatherland here, she thought, caring for your wives, your infants. But she knew that wasn't what the soldier meant.

She and Sister Columba — and any of the other Sisters left alive — were the ones who must march now. March along the streets, march to the death trains, to the labour camps from which no one ever returned.

She looked at the soldier with the bloody bayonet, and saw the hate that pulsed in him. She felt it spread to her too, its fire renewed.

All she could feel was hate.

Chapter 5

JOHANNES
POLAND, DECEMBER 1944

Christmas was coming, a time for stories!

The carol singers carried stars and performed scenes of Jesus's birth in the streets. Mutti and Lottie served hot almost-coffee and gingerbread.

Vati had not explained why the major had said Germany was doing bad things, horrible things. Instead he had met Mutti's eyes and shaken his head, then said quietly, 'We will not talk of this.' Later, in bed, Johannes heard them arguing in the living room below him. Vati had refused to admit the wife of the head of the local Nazi Party to their hospital. 'She just thinks she is sick! There are no signs of disease!'

'But wouldn't it be wiser …' began Mutti, and then her voice lowered, and Johannes couldn't make out any more.

But he heard no more arguments. And now it was nearly Christmas!

St Nicholas arrived on the night of his Feast day. He left books — books in German, and English too, for Vati and Mutti had studied in Edinburgh, which was where they met. One day they were going to take Johannes there too, but Edinburgh was in the land of the enemy now, so the visit would have to wait till Führer Hitler won.

The house smelled of gingerbread and happiness. Johannes helped Mutti and Lottie to cut Christmas dough into the shapes of deer and lambs and hearts to bake. They hung the tree with glass ornaments and painted eggshells, kept in tissue paper in the attic from year to year, and bright garlands, and Mutti placed the star on top.

The year before Vati had done that, but these days he had fewer doctors in his hospital, so he came home later and later at night, and in the mornings Mutti went to help too, or even stayed there overnight.

Johannes stood back to admire the tree, sparkling and gleaming, though the candles would not be lit till Christmas Eve. That was the tradition, but it was also necessary, for with the war there were few new candles to be had. 'Will Vati look at the tree before he goes to bed?' he asked Mutti.

'Of course!' said Mutti.

'Can I stay up until he comes home? Just for tonight?'

She smiled. 'Just for tonight.'

Lottie served supper then, roast rabbit from the rabbits on the hospital farm, with home-made noodles and vegetable soup. Johannes read in bed and tried to keep awake, listening for Vati's steps in the hall below, so he could run down and see Vati's face when he saw the Christmas tree.

He turned the pages, and more pages. More hours passed, and Vati didn't come.

At last he fell asleep.

Vati was not home at breakfast either.

'Stay home today,' Mutti said, putting on her fur coat, her white fur hat and her boots. 'I am sure it is nothing, just a little trouble at the hospital.'

Johannes played with Maus, then read a book, the one about the cow, which was too young for him now but made him remember Opa's voice. Was that what Opa meant by words cannot be burned?

Lottie served potato soup with specks of ham in it, but still Mutti did not return.

And then she did. Her lips were pale. Her eyes were dark. 'Vati has gone to Germany,' she said and tried to smile. 'It is an honour, a clever doctor like your father, to be invited to be a doctor in Germany.'

'But our hospital?' asked Johannes. 'Who will care for it now?'

'The German army needs the hospital for their soldiers,' said Mutti; Johannes could almost hear other words she didn't say.

'You mean it isn't ours now?'

'I ... I don't know. Perhaps one day, when the war is over.' Mutti tried to smile again. 'Yes, of course, when the war is over. But the German soldiers say we are allowed to join Vati now. We will have a big house, as big as this one. They say he is doing a most important job. We must take all our things, as much as we can carry. Our furniture will be sent to us.'

And so they packed, quickly. Two suitcases for Mutti, her jewels in one in a small locked case of their own; one suitcase for Johannes.

'Who will look after Maus?' he asked.

'Maus will stay here, and Lottie too, to look after the army doctor who will supervise the hospital. Just until the war is over,' said Mutti quickly. 'Then we will all come back and it will be just as it was before.' She didn't sound as uncertain now.

Lottie peered from the doorway. 'The master is not in any trouble, is he?' she asked quietly.

'How could he be, if we are told to join him?' replied Mutti. 'Besides, he has done nothing wrong. The soldiers say he has gone to a most important job. A secret one,' she added sternly to Lottie.

Johannes thought of the books hidden high on the shelves. What if the army doctor found them? But probably the army doctor would not want to read. The books would stay there, dusty, till they returned.

Soon they would be with Vati. In a city, perhaps, where there would be parades, as he had seen on a newsreel at the movie house when they had visited the town to order supplies. He might even see Hitler, standing on his balcony, saluting as the troops went past, the people cheering, and Johannes cheering too.

And Vati and Mutti would cheer on either side of him.

Chapter 6

JOHANNES
POLAND, DECEMBER 1944

A car came for them, a big car shining with importance. The soldier packed their suitcases in the back. Mutti's fingers glittered with her rings, and she wore her fur coat too. The car drove and drove, not to the station outside the village, but to another, a siding, away from houses, where cows and pigs were transported from the farms. A cattle train stood there already, topped with clean white snow, just like the snow on the siding.

The soldier helped them out. 'Your train will be here soon,' he said.

The car drove away.

They waited. Another car came, with neighbours, and then a truck, crammed with farm women and their children, and then another truck, followed by two more. 'This cannot be right,' said Mutti. She went to speak to a woman whose husband worked on the hospital farm, and then to two neighbours. When she came back, her face looked colder than the snow. 'Their men have all been sent to work too,' she said.

'But what about their farms? Their houses?'

'Other people are coming to work their farms.' She bit her lip. 'The whole village is being sent away. I should have brought the title deed to the hospital from the bank. Everyone has brought their valuables, but no one it seems has brought the deeds to their homes or farms. I ... I think I will ask if we can go tomorrow.'

Another truck drew up.

This one held soldiers, with rifles in their hands. 'Heil Hitler!' yelled the men. The women and children chorused, 'Heil Hitler!' in return.

Mutti approached a sergeant. 'Excuse me, my son and I need to stay a couple of days. There are matters I must attend to ...'

The sergeant did not seem to hear her. The soldiers opened the door of the cattle car.

'Excuse me,' repeated Mutti firmly, then stopped as the sergeant pointed his revolver at her, and then at Johannes. Mutti stared at the cattle car.

There was no other train coming. This train was not for cattle. It was for them.

Women cried. Protested. Mutti grabbed Johannes and pulled him back from the crowd. One of the soldiers fired a shot into the air.

The shouting stopped. The silence hung like a great blanket, broken only by the crying of a child.

The people moved, like cattle, into the car, dragging their suitcases, laying them on the floor, standing on them, for there was no other room. An old woman cried in pain, trying to force her bent body to stand straight, to take up less room.

'I think there has been a mistake,' said Mutti carefully to one of the soldiers. 'My husband is a doctor. So am I. We are to join him …'

'Inside! Macht schnell!' The soldier shoved Mutti away with the barrel of his rifle.

Mutti clambered in, trying not to show too much of her legs under her skirt, then turned to help Johannes. There was no room to sit. There was hardly room to stand. But still more bodies were pushed into the car. The soldiers pushed and shoved. Johannes heard three shots.

More jostles. The door shut, leaving them crushed in the dark and stink. The cattle car did not move.

It is a mistake, thought Johannes. It must be a mistake. Soon the right train will come, with a dining car and leather seats.

The cattle train began to rattle.

It kept on moving.

Hour on hour in darkness. A farm woman managed to open her case, and took out a chamberpot. Another woman held out her coat for privacy as the pot moved from hand to hand.

Then it was full, but there was no way to empty it, except trying to tip it from the small, high windows that breathed ice air. Some of the contents dribbled down the wall, then froze.

The cattle train kept moving.

And then it stopped. The door opened.

Snow scent. Snow light, blue bright, that ripped his eyes.

'Heil Hitler!' yelled men's voices. Johannes had to blink many times, and even then could only see them dimly, for the sharp light bouncing from the snow-covered trees blinded his eyes. Soldiers held up jugs of water. They held rifles too.

'Please …'

'Please …'

27

'My mother is ill ...'

'My aunt, my aunt is dying ...'

'Water. Please!'

'How much will you pay for the water?' asked a soldier.

Mutti held out a ring.

'More,' said the soldier. Mutti took off another ring and held it out too. Two rings for two jugs of water. It was not enough.

The thirsty women's faces stared at Mutti. The thirsty children's faces. Mutti bent and opened her case, and took out all her jewels. Jewels for water. No food, even for a pearl necklace. The woman with the chamberpot tried to empty it through the door, but a stick beat back her arm.

She dropped the pot.

'Heil Hitler!' yelled the soldiers. And then the door was shut.

The train moved again.

Women still cried then, and children. But soon they did not cry. No one had the strength to cry or speak.

Johannes tried to think. This was impossible. But it was real, so it must not be impossible.

Why was it happening? And how?

They had been kidnapped, he decided. Even though the soldiers cried 'Heil Hitler', they must have deserted. That was why they stole the jewellery. But Herr Hitler would not let the soldiers escape for long. Soon the train must stop, and the soldiers would be captured and punished. Herr Hitler would rescue everyone in the carriage, and all would be well.

Babies cried again, small canary cries, and then more weakly still. Then they did not cry at all. Women slumped, unconscious. They were so tightly packed no one could fall. Sometimes Johannes thought he slept. He dreamed he'd wake back in his bed.

But even before his eyes opened into blackness, he knew by the stench he was still there. At last he tried not to sleep, because the ogre came in the nightmares, the ogre that ate not just small boys but whole carriages of women and babies. At last there seemed no difference between sleeping and waking, for he knew the ogre stalked them, pacing along the railway tracks, his breath snorting like the engine of the train.

The boy in the book had saved everyone. But Johannes was not strong. They needed a true hero, like Herr Hitler. Surely the Führer would save them soon!

And then the train stopped. This time it didn't move again.

Chapter 7

JOHANNES
POLAND, DECEMBER 1944

The train doors stayed shut.

The living lay upon the dead, or almost dead. So many lay unmoving on the floor of the cattle car now that there was room for the others to sit, or stretch out slightly, although that meant lying on the dead. But there were so many now that they must either stand on or lie on them.

Johannes could feel Mutti's hand. It squeezed his, so he knew she was alive.

Time passed. A day? A night?

Back in the village, perhaps, they were eating the Wigilia supper, with carp and beetroot soup and gifts, and with hay on the table to remind them how Jesus was born in a stable and laid in a manger. Stories and songs around the Christmas tree. No, not in *their* village. In other villages.

But perhaps Christmas was past. Perhaps the ogre had eaten Christmas too ...

Sounds, doors sliding. An immense blanket of electric light. Light too bright to see. Light that swallowed colour, swallowed the world. Then Johannes saw beyond the light to night, darkness and barbed wire.

So much light, blue bright. So much barbed wire, grey and rusty red. A concrete railway platform, grey too, with puddles of fresh red and dried black. Dogs, giant German shepherds, laughing with red tongues lolling, like wolves in storybooks.

A few women tried to clamber from the cattle car. Men with machine guns gestured them back.

No one tried to leave the cattle car now, and at least the air smelled of snow, not death, or rather, death and snow.

Two skeletal men in faded rags brought buckets of water and two cups. The strongest or greediest women drank first. Mutti was one of the last, making sure Johannes drank before she did, then patiently trying to lift the heads of the almost-living so they could sip some water too.

The black sky turned to morning grey. The electric light switched off, leaving grey snow and greyer concrete.

Men marched to the platform. Grey men. Grey skin, grey rags flapping from arms as thin as children's. Skeleton men. They stood in rows.

An officer in green yelled, 'Heil Hitler!' Then, 'Get out!'

The women and children stumbled from the cattle car, most of the living, some helping the weak. The officer yelled, 'Come!'

The almost-living remained where they lay.

They will take the sick to hospital, thought Johannes. Because that was what happened when people were ill.

'Heil Hitler!' yelled the soldier again.

The crowd mumbled back, 'Heil Hitler.'

'Put down your suitcases. Do not try to carry anything with you. Move into rows. Five in each section. Move!'

Johannes moved.

Ambulances ploughed along the snowy road. They stopped. 'The ill will be taken to hospital,' said the soldier. Johannes felt the world shift slightly back into place. 'Doctors and nurses stand over there!'

Mutti moved, nodding to him as she stood with the nurses. The world still lurched to its right position. Doctors and nurses were needed for the sick. Soon he and Mutti would be with Vati ...

Mutti's line moved, each person stopping at a desk, showing their papers, then marching away to the side.

'Mutti!' called Johannes.

A guard jabbed him with his rifle, hard in the stomach. 'Quiet.'

The pain was ... just pain. After the forever in the cattle car, pain could be ignored. He forced himself to stand upright, so Mutti didn't think he was badly hurt. He tried to smile at her.

She turned to look at him. Don't speak, thought Johannes desperately. If Mutti called out, the guard might hit her too.

More trains drew up as they stood on the platform, and ghosts stumbled out.

Johannes stared. Were these truly people? Thinner even than the grey men, stooped, hunched, faces scared or desperate or simply staring. Soon the lines of ghost people stretched a long way beyond the station's platform, grey ghosts in white snow. One by one they stumbled to officers at a table, who looked at their wrists and checked off numbers, or merely glanced at them and waved them on, over to the right, to march and march, from the station through the snow.

The ghosts carried no suitcases. They almost looked as if they carried no life or hope either.

At last Johannes's line began to move. A soldier stared at Johannes. 'How old are you?'

He should have said, 'Ich bin zehn Jahre alt.' I am ten years old. Instead he asked, 'Why?'

'Children under twelve and old people go to the right. Men to the left.'

And the ghosts from the other trains, thought Johannes. All the ghosts had been sent to the right.

He should go with the other children. He should follow the ghosts to the right. But Mutti was in the line to the left.

'I am twelve years old,' said Johannes.

The soldier gestured to a rope stretched between two poles. 'Walk under that.'

Johannes stretched himself, trying to stand inconspicuously on tiptoe. 'I am too tall.'

'To the left,' said the soldier. A guard shoved him into a line with older boys, then hit him across the face when he edged to the side to see Mutti's line again.

Behind him, children screamed as they were forced into the line to the right. Mothers sent to the left shrieked and wailed. They held out hands to try to reach their children. The dogs growled, darted forwards, bit, then sat back, grinning at their SS masters.

More grey-faced men like the ones who had brought them water marched forwards. They lifted the dead out of the train and piled them on the platform. They lifted the women's suitcases with effort, and carried them away.

And still more cattle people turned to the right or left.

The air shuddered with children crying, 'Mutti!' or whimpering with pain. Some women sobbed, collapsing on the ground.

Mutti's line began to march. Once more she turned to him. Their eyes met. Mutti spoke, but not with words. Words in the

33

heart, thought Johannes, cannot be burned away. Even an ogre cannot swallow those. Mutti would find him. They would be together. He pushed the words deeper into his heart as she looked at him, making sure they were safe and could not leak away.

Mutti marched, with the other women, nurses and doctors, into the blankness of the snow.

Chapter 8

The boys marched in their groups of five, step by step along the snowy road. The air smelled faintly of old roasted meat, which should have made him hungry. But hunger was gone, and pain too, and even terror.

He just walked.

The light bounced from the snow. It was too bright. He looked for Mutti at first, but her line had vanished. He looked ahead instead.

The world in front of them was ringed by barbed wire, vast as a city. Giant cement posts held enormous eye-like lights. Inside the barbed wire, squares were marked off by snow and barbed wire-clad banks.

The gates opened. 'Heil Hitler!' shouted guards on each side of the great gate. Johannes's line marched inside.

Wooden buildings, each in its own cage. Skeletons in grey rags held out hands through the wire to the new arrivals, pleading for bread.

Lunatics, thought Johannes. That was why Vati and Mutti had been brought here. They need doctors to care for lunatics.

They waited. At last the doors of a giant shed opened. They marched inside.

'Heil Hitler!' barked a guard.

He waited till the line replied, 'Heil Hitler!'

'Undress!'

Guards yelled the order in many languages, German, Polish, English, others Johannes did not understand.

They undressed. They marched. They stood, naked, as guards clipped their hair. Johannes tried not to look; hoped no one looked at him. They showered. Each drop stung with ice.

Another room, piled with rags.

'Dress!'

A guard handed Johannes what had once been a shirt, grey as a duster. It reached down to his knees. Trousers, missing one leg, the other so long he had to roll it up. The letter 'P' was painted on his shirt. He supposed it stood for Poland.

The boys lined up outside again, barefoot now. The snow fell in soft wet handfuls. Pain, then numbness.

They marched. He could no longer feel his feet, but they still marched. A forest rose on either side, the green trees dappled with snow. The sun shone like a red ball, low on the horizon, below the snow clouds.

Somewhere in the real world it would be Christmas. Somehow, soon, he would be rescued and he would be in the real world again.

They marched past a red-brick building and the strange roasting smell was stronger: not like anything was cooking now,

36

but as if it had been cooked for a long while, some time ago — no smoke came from the chimneys. Great piles of logs were piled neatly on either side. A bakery, thought Johannes.

More barbed-wire gates. More giant electric eyes. The gates opened as the sun hid itself for the night.

They marched into a shed, divided into wooden cages, three wooden tiers in each. 'Heil Hitler!' yelled the guards who had escorted them.

Dim shapes called from the cages, 'Heil Hitler!'

The doors shut behind them.

And finally Johannes realised. This was the belly of the ogre, and there was no escape. For the ogre was called Hitler.

Chapter 9

Warmth. Or rather, cold that was not desperate, so he could think. His feet hurt, but it was good to feel them there again. If he opened his eyes, Mutti would be there …

He opened them. Saw wooden planks above his head. Two bodies moved either side. Boys, thin-faced, in rags worse than his own. Another rag of blanket covered him.

'Good,' said the older boy. 'He is awake.' He held out a hand, twisted and scarred, and touched Johannes's cheek gently. 'It is time to eat.'

'Eat,' snorted the other boy, sitting up. He slid off the wooden shelf and shuffled over to the door.

There was no room to sit up. The older boy said, 'Stay. Rest while you can. I'll bring your coffee.'

'I don't drink coffee.'

'That is good. Because it is not coffee, but it is warm and liquid. Listen!'

38

He did not want to listen. He wanted to drink warm not-coffee and then sleep.

The boy looked at him intently. 'Pay attention. You need to know things. If you do not, you will die.' The boy shrugged. 'Probably we will all die. But if you know things, you have a chance of life.'

Johannes forced himself to focus. This made sense. In every land there were new rules. New rules for the land called 'war'. New rules now in the ogre's belly. 'What must I know?' he whispered. 'Where are we?'

'We are in a camp at a place called Auschwitz. I used to be at the camp next door, Birkenau. It is a labour camp, a place where people are put to work, and work, and work. I worked in a factory making coats.' His face hardened. 'Others made fuses, or paints or enamelled pots. They became sick from the fumes.' He shrugged again. 'Then I was sent here.'

'Why?'

'I collapsed. This is where the weak are sent.' He grinned, showing gaps in his teeth and bloody red gums. 'But I am not ready to die.'

'Why didn't they send you to a hospital?' There must be a hospital, he prayed. A hospital where Mutti and Vati are working and safe.

The boy shrugged once more. 'It takes days, weeks, to be admitted to the hospital here. No, this is the place where people die. But if you are strong enough, you can still be chosen to do camp work and live. For a while.'

How could he be so cruelly matter-of-fact? Then Johannes saw his eyes. The boy was not cruel. Johannes too needed to know these things, if he was to live.

For a while.

The boy looked at Johannes assessingly. He said quietly, 'You are not twelve, are you?'

Johannes shook his head.

'Say you are twelve.'

'Why?'

The boy lowered his voice even more. 'I say this softly. If you are seen to know too much, you are taken out. Those who are taken do not come back.'

'They go home?' He knew as soon as he said it that it was stupid.

'They are killed,' said the boy flatly. 'You came here on a train?'

Johannes nodded.

'All of the people who went to the right at the station have been killed already: all the children, all the old or weak. Until a few months ago all Juden were burned in the ovens. Others were killed with injections or bullets or gas. Now?' He shrugged. 'I do not know what happens to the Juden now.'

'You mean they have stopped killing?'

'The killing goes on. Even more now, the killing goes on. But by starvation or ...' he glanced at Johannes's face, then added quietly, 'by other ways. Those who fail the labour selection at the parades are killed too. If you do not know enough, you may make a mistake.'

Johannes thought of the vast bakery they had passed, and deeply, horribly, knew it was all true. If he had turned to the right, he would be dead now too ...

'Stand straight at parade. Look down. Do not meet a guard's eyes. If you do, you will be whipped. If you are whipped, you may fall sick and die. Eat, drink, even if it is stinking. Work steadily. Do not ask questions. Do not do anything to make them notice you.'

40

Johannes nodded. He understood rules. These were the rules of the belly of the ogre.

'And live!' said the boy fiercely, as the other boy who'd shared their bunk brought over two bowls of some stinking brown stuff. He offered a bowl to the older boy, who shook his head. 'How long since you have eaten?' he asked Johannes.

'I don't know,' whispered Johannes.

Again the older boy shrugged. 'You can have my bowl too today.'

It was perhaps the most generous thing anyone had done for him. But you could not say that to other boys.

He looked around the barracks. Some of the newcomers sat sobbing on their bunks. No one had distributed food to them.

'Sometimes you need to fight to get your share,' said the older boy grimly. 'There is bread too, but the two of us are not strong enough to get any. Tomorrow you can help us. Those who work in the kitchens can hide food sometimes too.' He assessed Johannes again. 'Newcomers are strong. Perhaps you will be given kitchen work.'

Johannes sipped. The younger boy lay down again and seemed to drift to almost-sleep. The liquid was lukewarm, sour, like vomit left in a bucket. But he drank it all, felt his shrunken stomach rebel, clamped his mouth shut to force his stomach to keep it down.

'And remember,' said the older boy. 'Always remember: live!'

'How?' whispered Johannes. How could anyone live for long in this grey room, on this grey muck, as the cold draughts snapped and bit them on their bunks?

The boy looked at him steadily. 'There was a radio hidden in the coat factory. I never heard it, but the news from the BBC was whispered every day. The Allies are coming,' he said softly, and suddenly his eyes had hope. 'Soon the war will be over.'

'I ... I don't understand. Hitler is conquering the world.'

'Hitler is mad. All who follow him like slaves are mad.'

'Did the radio say that? The BBC is English. Maybe they lied.'

The older boy snorted. 'There are many in Poland and Germany who know the truth too, and were sent to the camps for saying it. There are others who know, but do not talk of it, try not to think of it.'

Johannes thought of the major, the words he spoke only when drunk. True words ...

'We are slaves here, but we are not mad, like those outside,' said the older boy. 'Soon — if we can live — we will be free.'

The boy gazed at Johannes with eyes that burned. 'Hitler took my family. Probably they are all dead by now. I do not know. But I know this. At night my hatred burns. My hatred keeps me warm.'

Chapter 10

FRAU MARKS
GERMAN-OCCUPIED POLAND
DECEMBER 1944

Frau Marks had been a nurse at the camp hospital for a little over a month. It was called a hospital. It was just another set of barracks, four or five hundred people on straw mattresses on wooden boards in the same bunks as the other barracks, but here at least there was one blanket for four people.

Most of the patients had been waiting days or weeks to be admitted. And so they died. Others were infectious, so must be taken to the infectious diseases ward to stop disease from spreading. There was no infectious ward, of course. The trucks that took the patients to the 'infectious ward' took them to death. But there was no choice, for to keep people with scarlet fever or typhus or tuberculosis among the rest was to risk everyone.

She looked down at the new arrival, shoved from the stretcher onto the wooden bunk. She wore a nightdress that covered only her torso. Her shiny bald head was bright red, as if it had been burned. Her skin was white in places, red in others.

Frau Marks had seen patients like this before. Radiation experiments, one of the many kinds performed on prisoners here.

She knew too there was nothing she could do. No cure, not even any way to ease the awful pain. She turned, to others whom she might just possibly be able to help by seeing they drank till their fever burned away or their wounds healed — not much chance, but a little — when the whisper came.

'My dear Nurse Stöhlich.'

Frau Marks turned back and saw Sister Columba's smile in that ravaged face.

She had not cried since she'd come here. Tears were a waste of her body's fuel and energy. She must stay alive for Georg. But now she knelt and wept.

'What have they done to you?' She shook her head. 'No, do not tell me,' she whispered, 'I know.'

Dr Mengele liked nuns for his experiments. The guards enjoyed humiliating them, stamping on their crucifixes, lashing them with whips, ordering the big dogs to attack and laughing as they did.

'I ... cannot help you,' Frau Marks whispered. Sister Columba deserved to know the truth. 'I don't even have any morphia to help with the pain.'

'You can pray for me, as I will pray for you.' The old eyes met hers. 'God is here.'

Was He? Frau Marks didn't know. But she could not say that to Sister Columba now.

Chapter 11

FRAU MARKS
GERMAN-OCCUPIED POLAND
DECEMBER 1944

The order came on New Year's Eve. There had been another 'selection' on parade, this time of young people — the youngest ones still alive after the initial sorting at the station. The new order said that these older children were to be washed by some of the nurses and doctors of the barracks shed they called the hospital.

It was such an innocent request.

Frau Marks looked at the lines of children, looked at their thin bare arms in their grey rags. None wore the tattoos reserved for registered members of the camp. The tattoos were painful, and often became infected. Hers was still swollen, though she tried to keep it clean. But the tattoos meant *some* security — being registered meant that you were useful to keep alive. For a while.

The children marched. Hundreds of them, barefoot, thin and tattered, along the Lagerstrasse to the showers. The snow had melted, but the road had turned to ice. Frozen feet turned blue then red as that ice cut them like knives. And still they marched, child after child.

Frau Marks and the other nurses marched beside them.

At first the children cried, and then they whimpered. Then even the strength for that was gone. The children marched in silence, staggering, knowing that to stop was certain death.

'Why?' whispered Frau Marks. 'Why?'

She did not expect an answer, but one came from a nearby guard. He leered at her, waiting to see if she might smile at him, flirt with him, in exchange for a piece of bread, or sausage. But she did not. He shrugged. 'There are too many brats. Too young to be of use. They must be got rid of.'

'But they are going to be bathed ...' She meant: They are not going to the gas chambers.

He shrugged again. 'They are not jüdisch.' Jüdische children of all ages were gassed as soon as they arrived. 'One of the higher-ups suggested they be put into a pit and burned, but gasoline is precious. So are bullets.'

'But they are just to be bathed!'

He laughed in his boots and overcoat. 'Water is cheap.'

A child fell. The whip came down, splattering red. Two children bent to help the fallen one up.

They staggered on.

Another child fell. Frau Marks ran to help. The guard forced her back.

It began to snow. Flakes like plates, drifting down so gently onto the crumpled tiny bodies of the children on the ground.

They reached the showers. 'Haltet hier! Halt!'

One by one, the nurses bathed the children, boys with ribs like xylophones, girls with wrists like chicken legs. Children who did not moan or weep, even when the icy water lashed them.

There was no soap. No towels.

'Dress them!'

The nurses dressed the children back in their rags, still wet.

They marched out to roll call, nurses, wet children, onto ground of ice, into air of snow.

They waited, standing in their lines.

One hour, two. Frau Marks had thought she could not cry again. She cried now.

The children died, one by one, in threes and fours, collapsing in the snow.

Three hours. Four. Some children still stood to attention in the snow. More fell. More died. And more.

Five hours. A bored guard strolled beside the few children still standing in the lines, slashing at their faces with his whip, leaving some, choosing others, perhaps only on a whim, until they fell. No one was allowed to touch them. Each child lay till cold stole the last of the life within them.

She did not think she could stand. She did not think she could live.

Georg. She blinked and tried to bear the agony, the cold. She must live for him.

And finally the order, 'March!'

Miraculously, a few children still stood, tottering. Miraculously, they marched, one step, or ten. Then fell. But the nurses were permitted to catch them now.

A boy fell beside her. A boy Georg's age. No, younger: the age her son had been the last time she had seen him. She caught the child before he slumped into the snow. He was surprisingly heavy. Vaguely she supposed he must be new, not yet starved to stick-like thinness. A faint hope prickled, so very, very faint. Maybe, just maybe, this boy might survive.

Each nurse carried a child now, for there were no stretchers. Skeleton children, who must weigh little, which was good, because most of the nurses had been here far longer than she had, and so were weaker. She was glad that she was the one who had the heaviest burden. Step by step the nurses struggled, carrying the children, the precious few children, through the snow.

How many children had died that day? She did not know. How many died on this march back to the barracks? Hundreds? Had anyone even counted them?

She looked down at the boy in her arms. He breathed, although his eyes were shut. She glanced at the nurse behind her, and briefly shut her eyes in grief. The girl the other woman was carrying had died, but how could she in all compassion tell the nurse to put the child down?

At last they reached the hospital barracks. She watched as the nurses piled the bodies they carried behind the shed, for the rats to eat that night. The boy she held still lived, his breathing harsh and faint.

She held him to her and stumbled inside the shed they called a hospital. She laid him on a bunk.

Yes, he was still alive. The faint hope grew stronger.

A woman, still a woman, was standing in the doorway, with a layer of flesh and fat that said she was new, as did the shock that showed on her face as she watched the nurses lay the children's bodies in the pile, and the few nurses who carried live children struggle inside with them. 'We have to get them warm,' she ordered, her voice blank with horror.

'How?' asked someone wearily.

'Hold them to you,' said the new doctor desperately. 'Two or three of you. Your body heat will warm them ...'

What heat? thought Frau Marks tiredly. But she moved the boy to beside Sister Columba, then laid herself on the other side of him. They wrapped what life they still had about him, as the new doctor cajoled the starving nurses to give their almost-hot mugs of evening soup to the children.

The boy's eyes opened. Frau Marks forced herself to smile at him. 'Rest,' she whispered. 'I am Nurse Stöhlich.' Her false name was automatic now.

The doctor brought a mug of soup. Frau Marks helped the boy sit up so she could hold the mug for him, while he sipped. Keep him warm, give him food. Maybe, maybe he would live …

The doctor stared at the boy, and then she almost fell across the bed to get to him. 'Johannes!' The new doctor clasped the boy, then gazed at Frau Marks, her face ripped by anguish. 'This is my son.'

Chapter 12

JOHANNES
GERMAN-OCCUPIED POLAND
JANUARY 1945

Dreams slashed him. The ogre thudding after him through snow that burned; he reached up to the forbidden books at home, but when he touched one it ate his fingers, then his arm. He tried to scream —

'Sshh. Sshh, child.' He opened his eyes. He was on the lowest of the bunks. A woman lay next to him. Or was she a woman? For she had no hair. Her eyes were red, as if she had wept blood. Her face was very white, except where it was blistered red. Her blistered hand stroked his cheek. 'Do not be frightened.'

That was so stupid the dream vanished, and its terror too. 'Why not?'

The woman — yes, she was a woman, her voice was a woman's — said, 'Because there is love here.'

Here, in the belly of the ogre? He shook his head. 'No,' he managed.

'Oh, yes. God loves you. And I love you. We have become friends, you and I, though you did not know it. I have held you, and you kept me warm. I prayed for you, and praying for you meant I was with God, not here.'

Her words made no sense. And then she added, 'Your mother loves you too.'

He shook his head, confused. He had dreamed Mutti was here. 'I thought I saw her ...'

'Sshh. Save your strength. You saw her. Your mother is a doctor here. She has gone to fetch the food buckets. Ah, here she is.'

Mutti, carrying the buckets of ditchwater that was soup. She put them down carefully as the nurses brought the bowls to fill, and crouched down by the bunk. 'I didn't think ... I was so afraid ...' She shook her head, then held him instead.

She smelled of sickness and rotting skin and ditchwater soup. She smiled like Mutti. He tried to hug her back and found his arms had turned to marzipan.

Mutti sat back. 'Sshh. Do not try to move. You must keep your strength. Sister Columba?'

The woman next to him shuffled painfully upright. She waited till Mutti placed Johannes in her arms. 'Drink,' said Mutti, handing Sister Columba a bowl of soup, lifting another for him to drink.

'You take my share,' said Sister Columba to Johannes, as the boy had told him on his first night.

'You must eat too,' Mutti told her.

'Must I?' Sister Columba smiled. 'You and I both know what my end will be here. I have few choices here, my dear. Do not deprive me of one of those left to me.' She reached up with blistered hands to help steady the bowl for Johannes.

He felt better when he had drunk the bowls of soup, chewing the shreds of turnip at the bottom. He felt sleepy, grateful when Mutti eased him down. 'This is Nurse Stöhlich,' said Mutti as a tall woman with blonde tufts of hair on her scalp appeared by the bunk. 'She carried you back, out in the snow. She or I and Sister Columba will always be with you.'

He could not remember Nurse Stöhlich. Or could he? 'I have a son the same age as you — or he was the same age, once,' said Nurse Stöhlich.

Everyone had been the same age once. But he did not have the strength to tell her.

'Sleep,' said Mutti.

He shut his eyes, then opened them. 'Vati?'

'I do not know. Not in the men's camp, I think.'

'But the soldiers said ...' He did not know if he said the words, or just thought them. This world had no truth, so why would Vati be at the same place they had been sent to, just because the Germans had said he would?

'I must see to other patients,' said Mutti softly. 'I will be back.'

He didn't want her to go. She had no right to go! She had left him once. She must stay with him, now, not go to 'other patients'.

'I want gingerbread,' he whispered, knowing he sounded like a little child, not caring. Christmas was over and there had been no gingerbread or baked carp, and Mutti had left him, and Opa and Vati ...

Mutti looked like she might cry. 'Johannes, I will try to get you what I can. But gingerbread is not possible.'

'I will give him gingerbread,' said the scarred nun beside him. 'Settle down, child, and listen.'

'Gingerbread ...' whispered Johannes. But speaking was too much work.

The frail woman smiled up at Mutti and nodded slightly, then turned to him. 'Once there was a whole land made of gingerbread. Not just the house but the forest and the earth. Gingerbread flowers grew in the gardens and gingerbread cats chased gingerbread mice. And then one day ...' she paused dramatically, 'it rained! You know what happens to gingerbread when it rains?'

Johannes smiled and shut his eyes. The gingerbread would turn to ginger mud. The ginger cat would never catch the ginger mouse ...

Vaguely he heard, 'When you wake up, I will tell you how my mother stole the cherry jam when she was just your age. She was naughty, but it is a funny story and, oh, that jam, the best you have ever tasted. There will be roast potatoes in that story too, as well as gingerbread ...'

Chapter 13

When you had stories about roast pork and apple sauce and how the dog had wriggled its nose up onto the table and dragged the roast away, and Sister Columba's mother and father and sisters and brothers all ran after it, and how there had been sausages instead for supper ... when you had stories like that, lying almost warm inside her arms, you could wait longer for real food.

'Here.' Mutti smiled, for she had a treat for him that day: bread with a thin scrape of margarine, and cheese! Real cheese. He nibbled it, as if he were a mouse, tried not to see the envious eyes of others watching him eat.

Sister Columba watched too. She had not told him a story that day, had hardly moved at all, though her lips moved silently as she gazed up at the bunk above.

Johannes blinked. 'Mutti, what is that smell?'

'The SS are burning the camp records,' said Mutti flatly.

'Why?'

She bent closer and whispered. This, it seemed, was one of the dangerous things to know, or talk about. 'The Russian soldiers are close. If you listen, you will hear explosions. I think they want to hide what they have been doing here.'

The boy who had given him his coffee the first day had said the war was nearly over. Had he been right?

He must be dead, Johannes realised, and the second boy too. There hadn't even been time to know their names.

'You mean ... we will soon be free?'

Mutti nodded. 'Yes,' she said. But she did not sound sure.

Yells came from outside. Guards marched through the door. 'All medical equipment must be brought out the front at once!'

Mutti stepped forwards. 'But we need ...'

'Silence!'

Johannes clenched his fists in fear until Mutti stepped back. Didn't she know she must not look the guards in the face? She must not let them notice her?

To his relief the guards didn't strike her with their rifles. They simply left, as if they had more important things to do.

The senior doctor nodded to Mutti to begin collecting the equipment, the bowls and the few syringes and tubing.

Johannes finished his bread and cheese. He slept, for he was still weak. Sister Columba still seemed mostly asleep. Voices yelled and screamed and whimpered, but those were noises of every day. His body had taught him to sleep through noises like those.

He woke to Mutti's hands. 'Johannes, Johannes, wake up!'

He struggled out of the deep snow bank of sleep. 'Mutti?'

'They are taking the doctors and nurses away. We must march. The Russian soldiers are coming.'

He began the dark journey to sit up. Her hands pressed him down. 'Only the doctors and nurses,' she said, her voice breaking. 'The patients must stay here.'

'No!'

'I would take you too, if I could. But they would see right away you are too young to be a doctor.' She lowered her voice still more. 'I will escape. Nurse Stöhlich and I, together. We have a plan. I will come back for you.'

He clutched her. 'Mutti, I —'

Johannes had not seen the guard. He grabbed Mutti by a tuft of hair. Mutti screamed, then held the scream back and struggled to her feet. She gazed back at Johannes.

'I love you!' her lips formed, but she did not say the words, in case the guard noticed, in case he killed them both.

He swung his legs off the bed to run after her, to at least watch her march away. Sister Columba's blistered hand grabbed his arm. It was a thin hand, and it must have cost her agony to touch things, but all her remaining strength was in it. 'Stay.'

'But Mutti —'

'If you call out to her, they may kill her, just to see you cry. Or kill you, to punish her. Stay.'

'But what will happen to us?'

'Johannes, you must listen to me. You have to hide. Now.'

'But —'

'Sshh.' He could feel her pulling together every thread of strength. 'Soon the guards will come to kill us. Kill every one of us so no one can tell those who win the war what monsters the Nazis have been. That is why they burned the records, why they have marched the doctors and nurses away. Go, now! I will pray for you,' she added.

'I ... I do not want to leave you.' Not to die alone, he thought.

She had given him gingerbread and roast potatoes, and her arms and warmth.

'Pray for me. Live for me. But go, quickly, while the guards are busy with the medical people.'

He hesitated, kissed her cheek. She winced as if even that gentle pressure hurt. She had been hugging him the past two weeks. How much had that hurt her too?

No time to think. 'I love you,' he said, because that was all he had to give, and he had forgotten to tell Mutti.

But Mutti knew. Surely she knew?

He put his feet onto the floor. He had no shoes, only his grey rag of nightgown ... but a pair of boots had been left by the door, flapping at the sole. They were too big, but he put them on and slipped out the door.

It was as if his body knew where to hide, even if his mind could not accept it. He ran towards the pile of bodies behind the barracks, the land of rats.

Chapter 14

She had never seen Dr Wolcheki weep, but she wept now, gazing back at the barracks door behind which Johannes lay. Johannes, so like Georg ...

No. Georg was older. And safe. He must be safe!

She put her arms around Dr Wolcheki as they stood, hour after hour, in their lines in front of the barracks. Flames leaped and snickered from vast piles of burning records all across the camp as darkness seeped around them.

Gunfire rumbled in the distance. Explosions snorted great gleams of red and yellow snot into the air. The light from the burning records was too bright to let the stars shine, but now and then the sky was ripped apart by fireworks. No, not fireworks ... warworks ... She forced her mind alert.

At last they moved, thousands of women, the doctors and the nurses first, and then other prisoners, shuffling towards the camp's barbed-wire gates, then stopping. Thirty guards stood at the gates. Frau Marks watched as nurses and doctors in front of her were examined one by one, by torchlight. Nurse Strzelecki was roughly shoved back to the camp: her hands were ulcerated, as were her feet. She would not be able to march far. The guards knew it.

Another reject. And another. For the first time Frau Marks allowed herself to hope. If the weak and ill were being left here to die, then the doctors and nurses and others from the camp must be going to a place where, just possibly, they might live.

She thought of Nurse Strzelecki. Of Sister Columba. Of Johannes. Of all her patients too weak to leave, left in the bunks. Guilt closed her throat so that, for a moment, she could not breathe. Beside her, she felt Dr Wolcheki tremble. 'Perhaps they will send me back to the hospital too,' she whispered, glancing back at the hospital hut hopefully.

Not after only three weeks in hell, thought Frau Marks. Dr Wolcheki was the strongest of them all.

Frau Marks stepped forwards, stood obediently looking down as the torchlight shone into her face, along her body. Hands shoved her onwards, and Dr Wolcheki too.

She grabbed Dr Wolcheki's hand. 'He will hide. He is a clever boy, your Johannes.' But Sister Columba could not hide. Impotent rage flooded her. A woman who had done so much good, to be killed by so much evil. The least she deserved was not to die alone.

Her mind stilled, even as her body shuffled forwards with the others. She could hear Sister Columba's laugh, the soft one of joy she gave at each new birth. 'But I am not alone. I am with God.'

The road turned. Dr Wolcheki looked back, yearningly. Frau Marks looked back too, in hatred, and in hope.

The SS guards surrounded them as they marched along the Auschwitz road. The snowy air felt like shards of glass each time she breathed. More rockets lit the skies, red and yellow and strange streaks of metal blue. The screams and thumps of battle sounded closer.

She had been trained to save lives, had spent her adult life doing just that. And yet now she felt a deep and savage glee. Let the Russians kill every SS man, every Nazi, everyone who cheered for Hitler, everyone who looked away as the death trains passed their homes …

'Schnell! Schnell!' Faster! Faster! The guards fired shots, urging the prisoners to run. The big German shepherd dogs ran beside the columns, snarling, nipping at legs, ankles, to make sure they all stayed in line.

Sweat ran down beneath her clothes. Women collapsed into small shaking heaps. A woman in front of her stumbled, raised her hands in a silent plea towards a guard. The guard pointed his revolver.

Crack. The woman fell, dark blood in a dark night.

Bodies tumbled into the ditches along the road.

How many of us can survive this? thought Frau Marks.

And then she realised. This was not a march to safety, to work in a hospital for wounded soldiers as she had hoped. This march was just another cheap, efficient mass murder. Like the children's washing, where no gas, no kerosene, no bullets or lethal injections had been wasted. The SS had no intention of leaving anyone alive who might tell what they had done. This way the bodies would be scattered along the roadways, with no piles of corpses to hide.

Daylight crept under the fierce light of flames and rockets. The women still stumbled along. The guards took turns riding in horse-drawn carts, but even the horses were exhausted, plodding with dull, sunken eyes and stick ribs.

Through villages, some shredded into matchsticks by the bombs, others strangely untouched by war or death, neat curtains at neat windows, neat trees in neat gardens, but no people to be seen. Either the villages were deserted, or the inhabitants had decided the line of marching dead should not be seen.

A forest, a farmhouse nestled into trees. Another village, then another. Night gathered around them again. The beat of war seemed neither nearer nor further behind them.

'Halte dort an!' Stop there!

A barn. The women in her group stumbled towards it. No hay. A pungent stink of cows, but the animals this barn had sheltered were gone. Frau Marks dropped upon the ground next to Dr Wolcheki, plunged into what was partly sleep, partly black exhaustion of mind and body.

Shots just outside the barn woke her. She raised her head and looked around. The other women slept, or were unconscious. The guards dozed too, except for one.

If she and Dr Wolcheki did not escape soon, then they would die. If they tried to escape, they would probably die too, but at least that way they had hope, could die in defiance, not just in fear.

She touched Dr Wolcheki's shoulder lightly, felt her instantly alert, whispered, 'We must escape. Now.'

She felt rather than saw Dr Wolcheki nod. Of course she would escape if there was the slightest possible chance it might take her back to Johannes.

Frau Marks tried to calculate. They could probably make it out the doors and to the trees before the dozing guards could aim their machine guns at them. But the guard by the door would fire at them as soon as he saw them move …

Yells, outside. Shots. Other women were escaping. Or dying as they escaped?

She did not know. Did not have time to think. She grabbed Dr Wolcheki's hand as their guard ran towards the noise outside. Together they plunged at the door.

Clean night air. No time to stop. Trees, night-shadowed forest, to the left. They ran, heads down, not looking to either side. Shots, and more shots. She heard Dr Wolcheki gasp. Bullets cracked around them.

Trees! Their shadows gathered them and hid them, but they still ran, for bullets snickered all around. A mound of snow … She pulled Dr Wolcheki down behind it as more bullets snickered above.

Blood bloomed on the snow, a red flower on Dr Wolcheki's dress. 'Can you go on?'

Dr Wolcheki pressed a hand to her bloody side. She nodded.

They crawled along the snow bank, keeping their heads down. Crawled and crawled …

Footsteps, running towards them. And suddenly she knew she had no more strength left to run. She waited for the death shots.

A voice said, 'Go to the house on the left. Hurry!'

She looked up. An elderly man in ragged farmer's clothes, his boots held together with twine, peered down at the two women. 'Hurry!' he whispered. 'The Germans are in the village. Head for the barn behind the house.' He hesitated, then added, 'If you are caught, I have not seen you. Tell them no one in the house knows you are there. You understand?'

'I understand,' muttered Frau Marks. A good man. But he must think of his family too.

Dr Wolcheki slumped unconscious beside her. The farmer swore, under his breath, as Frau Marks tried and failed to lift her. The farmer bent to help.

They dragged the unconscious woman towards the barn.

Chapter 15

JOHANNES
GERMAN-OCCUPIED POLAND
14 JANUARY 1945

Trucks rumbled under bright electric light, all through the night, lined up waiting for the guards at the gate to check the drivers' papers, taking people and equipment away into the darkness beyond the barbed wire. At last Johannes moved, a thin shadow, towards a line of trucks that idled as the guard looked at the drivers' papers. He grabbed onto a truck, managed to climb up its side, then clambered under the tarpaulin.

The truck was filled with suitcases. He wriggled into a space among them, then felt the vehicle move, the bump of wheels and the occasional skid on the icy road.

He wanted to look out to try to see the marching women, but the guards might notice movement under the tarpaulin. Nor could he hear the shouts of guards that would mean the marchers were nearby.

Hours passed. Days? He dozed from exhaustion, and had no way to tell.

At last the truck stopped. He peered out from under the tarpaulin. It was still night, and probably the same night he had left. He slipped out, down onto the snow, glad of his too-big boots. His legs did not work properly, nor his arms. He forced himself to move. In among the trees, then deeper, into the forest, the tree trunks dark on dark.

There was a light, a single candle. He moved towards it. There was a door. And knowing he could not keep moving, and that if he lay to sleep in the snow he would never wake, he knocked, not with hope, but because he could see no choice.

The door opened. A woman stared at his grey rags, the letter 'P'. 'Jude!' The woman's word was a grunt.

'Nein! Nicht Jude!'

'Go! We don't want your sort here!'

'Grossmutti, he is just a boy!'

'A boy who will bring us trouble!'

The other voice sounded both scared and weary. 'The Russians will bring us more trouble than a boy.'

Hands reached out, pulling him inside. Soup, made of potatoes and cabbage, thin, but the first proper food he had eaten since home. A bench by a fire, a feather-filled quilt, and true warmth. And around him, two women bustling and a child crying.

And sleep.

Chapter 16

JOHANNES
GERMAN- AND RUSSIAN-OCCUPIED POLAND
15 JANUARY 1945

He woke to a thunderstorm, kind hands and more soup. The younger woman's voice said, 'Drink it quickly. You must get dressed.' She thrust clothes at him. 'These were my son's.'

Were. Her son must be dead.

The woman said hurriedly, 'We must get to the train station. The Russians will be here soon.'

Johannes suddenly realised that the thunder must be shelling, like the noises he had heard at the movie house.

His hands trembled, but he dressed himself in the unknown boy's clothes. He joined the old woman, who glared at him crossly. The younger woman carried a baby girl.

Outside it was late afternoon. They walked, the old woman carrying two suitcases, the younger woman one suitcase and the child, through the trees, then through a village. He wanted to ask their names, but thought: If they capture us, I must pretend I do not know them.

But no one would know he came from the camp now that he was dressed in proper clothes. He was in no more danger than these women.

Nor any safer.

Thunder screamed about them. Someone shouted, 'In here!' They scurried through a doorway, down a ladder, into a cellar dark with the scent of fermenting jam.

Noise grew till it was impossible to tell one explosion from the next. The universe was noise. Johannes covered his ears, to block out the bombs, the screams, the memories. Did Mutti have a cellar to hide in? Warm clothes, like he had, and food? Was she still marching?

Time passed. So did the night. At last a square of light appeared. The cellar door, opening.

One by one the villagers climbed up to the surface. He could not see the two women and the child he had arrived with. Perhaps they did not want him to see them, so didn't meet his eyes.

The cottage above them was shattered sticks, a window, a dead cat. He thought of Maus, but could not cry.

They were a mob now, thirty villagers perhaps, mostly women, children, a few old men, running-walking along the road. No one asked who he was. A railway station. Carriages, true carriages, not cattle cars. It was impossible to fit everyone in.

They did.

He lay across the laps of two farm women. Big fat laps, and warm. For some reason it hurt to breathe. Again he slept.

He woke to find the world was slipping in and out of blackness. He thought: I have a fever. I am ill. Breathing hurt so much the world went black.

And then he thought nothing, except dreams.

Chapter 17

JOHANNES
GERMANY, LATE JANUARY 1945

And then the dreams stopped.

Johannes knew they had stopped because the girl who sat beside him was not like anyone he had seen before, not in a dream or a nightmare.

She was small, his age perhaps. She was strange too. It took him a moment to work out what the strangeness was. Not the mark on her face — that might be a bruise or a burn — but that she was ... not fat, but not thin either. How long in this ogre's world had it been since he had seen a girl who was not thin?

And then he realised something else: he could breathe. It still hurt to breathe too deeply. But air went in and air went out without the world turning black again. He could almost hear Mutti say, 'This is good.'

Mutti! He had to find her. And Vati. Or they had to find him.

The girl held a spoon and a cracked cup of water. Johannes felt his moist lips. She must have been spooning water drip by drip into his mouth as he lay unconscious. That is what Mutti and Nurse Stöhlich and the others had done when people were unconscious back in the camp, so they did not die from lack of water while their bodies were trying to recover. Often it was all that they could do to help them. But it could save lives.

Perhaps this girl had saved his.

He managed to look around. A barn, piled with hay. He lay on a blanket on the hay, with another blanket over him, the hay fluffed up to help keep him warm. A little way away a thin woman lay on blankets in the hay too. She muttered as she slept. A boy, thin too, about eight years old, sat next to the woman, holding her hand.

'What happened? Where am I?' he whispered.

'I am Helga Schmidt,' said the girl, which wasn't what he'd asked.

'I am Johannes. Johannes Wolcheki.'

The girl nodded. 'This is my brother, Hannes.'

The smaller boy nodded a greeting. 'I am really Johannes too. But I like Hannes better.'

'And this is our mother, Frau Schmidt,' said Helga.

'Do you live here?'

'In a barn? Of course not,' said the boy, Hannes. 'We live in a big house, in Berlin.' His face twisted. Johannes could see he was trying not to cry. 'But then the tanks came. We hid in the cellar, but the Russian soldiers found us. They hurt Mutti and Helga —' He stopped and corrected himself. 'They hurt Mutti. So we ran and hid, and H-Helga had a pass that got us on a train ...'

Johannes tried to follow the boy's story, turning to the girl for clarification. 'Did the soldiers hurt you? The bruise on your face looks bad.'

'I was born with the mark on my face. It's called a birthmark,' said Helga quietly. 'The soldiers didn't hurt me.'

'Helga,' moaned Frau Schmidt. 'Do not hurt Helga! Please! Please, stop!'

'Mutti!' Hannes bent to her again. 'Wake up! Helga is here. Safe. See?'

Frau Schmidt woke. She had been sleeping, Johannes realised with relief, not unconscious as he had been. But one side of her lips was purple and swollen, and a dribble of blood ran from the corner of her mouth. Helga crawled over to her, took a damp rag and wiped away the blood. Frau Schmidt blinked at her.

'See,' Hannes said clearly. 'Mutti, here is Helga.'

'Helga?' said Frau Schmidt. Then she nodded. 'Yes, Helga. We … we are so blessed that Helga is here for us.'

It was … odd. But this was the world of odd.

'Soldiers stopped the train …' Frau Schmidt did not say if they were German or Russian. They all knew that in this world soldiers took what they wanted.

'We ran,' explained Hannes, 'and Helga saw you, curled up under a bush. She said you were ill and needed help. She and I carried you here.' Hannes's voice was proud.

Johannes tried to think. He had a vague memory — or was it a dream? The women in the train had thought he was ill. He *was* ill. But they thought it might be an illness that would infect them too, like typhus or scarlet fever. There had been arguing, rough hands, yelling, a woman crying. Children crying, whimpering, which this world was full of, except here in the sanctuary of the barn, where the only noise was the far-off thunder.

Not thunder. War.

He must have staggered a little from where the villagers had dumped him, out of the train.

Helga said, 'We have some food. Can you eat now?'

He sat up, supported by the hay. Yes, he could eat.

'Helga found a cheese,' said Hannes proudly. 'The house was wrecked, but Helga crept in, just like a mouse.'

A mouse ran by behind him, then stopped, its nose quivering as if it had heard the word 'cheese'.

Johannes laughed, then stopped. How could he laugh here?

'What's funny?' asked the boy, Hannes.

He pointed. Helga turned to look too. She smiled at the mouse, so small, so hopeful. Hannes laughed too. Even Frau Schmidt smiled.

Helga burrowed under the hay. There was the cheese, wrapped in layers of cloth to keep the mice from it. There were other packages too, and three jars of what looked like jam. Helga opened one of the jars. She handed him the spoon and then the jar. It was plum, he thought, from its colour.

'I can't eat all your jam,' he said awkwardly.

'Eat a third of it. Hannes can have the rest and Frau — and Mutti.'

'Helga.' Frau Schmidt said her daughter's name as carefully as Helga had said 'Mutti'. 'You must eat too.'

'Helga won't eat,' said Hannes.

'I don't need food as much as you do.' It was evident she had said it many times before. 'See?' She held up her well-fleshed wrist. Her coat was good, Johannes noticed, not faded and worn thin like every garment he had seen in these last years of war. Its pockets bulged.

His hand trembled as he spooned the jam. Cherry jam, not plum. It tasted like home. Helga, Hannes and Frau Schmidt pretended not to see his tears.

He could have eaten twenty jars. Instead he carefully stopped when he had eaten a quarter of it. Helga took the jar and handed it to Hannes.

'No,' said Hannes stubbornly. 'You eat.'

'No ... I ...' Helga stopped, shrugged, took the jam. She dipped in the spoon and raised it to her mouth, though the level of the jam did not get any lower. After a while she passed it to Hannes.

Johannes thought Hannes hadn't noticed. He ate ravenously, but stopped too, to hand the last of the jam to his mother.

'And now the cheese,' said Helga. She used the spoon as a knife, ten spoonsful for each of them. Johannes watched her hesitate, then eat four spoonsful herself. Did she know exactly how little she could eat, and still look after them?

The cheese was wonderful. It was just cheese, real cheese. No maggots, no bitterness, no mould, buttery and rich.

'Sleep,' said Helga to Johannes and Frau Schmidt. She peered out the door at the growing dusk. 'I'll go and get some water. The well is just over there. Hannes, you keep watch.'

'Be careful,' said Frau Schmidt fretfully. 'Remember how they hurt Helga.'

'Mutti, this is Helga,' said Hannes loudly.

Frau Schmidt blinked. 'I am sorry,' she whispered to Johannes. 'I ... I am confused. It has been a ... a hard time.'

'Yes,' said Johannes. 'It's been hard.'

71

Chapter 18

It was quiet and dark when Helga returned, limping slightly, a bucket in one hand, another cloth-wrapped parcel in the other, something bulky strapped onto her back. Hannes slept, cuddled next to Frau Schmidt.

'I told Hannes to sleep,' whispered Johannes. 'I have slept enough.'

'You're sick. You need to sleep more. But I think we can stay here for a few days till you are stronger, and Frau — and *Mutti* also. If any soldiers come, we can cover ourselves with hay, but this village has been bombed so badly it's deserted. I don't think soldiers will bother with it. Look!' She held up four blankets, then tenderly covered Hannes and Frau Schmidt with two of them and handed one to Johannes. She wrapped herself in the other, like a shawl, then offered him water from the bucket.

He drank. It was pure and fresh, the best water he had ever drunk. Helga handed him a shrivelled apple. He ate that too. At last she asked, 'Where are you going?'

'I don't know. To find Mutti and Vati.'

'Where are they?'

'I ... I don't know.' The world suddenly seemed very large. 'Hitler took them to work, because they are doctors, because the soldiers wanted our hospital. Maybe ... maybe they are going home.'

'Where is home?'

He told her. She shook her head. 'That is in Poland. The Russians are there.'

'That is good, isn't it? That means the Germans have gone. Vati can have his hospital back again and we will have our house.'

Helga looked thoughtful. 'I think you should stay with us. Not go near the Russians.'

'Why?'

'Because they are very angry,' said Helga simply. 'Because our soldiers, the Germans, killed their soldiers even after they surrendered. Because German soldiers did terrible things to Russian people, so the Russians do the same to us.'

How did she know these things? But she seemed very sure. 'Hate is like a bacterium,' said Johannes. 'It spreads. Nurse Stöhlich told me that,' he added. 'She worked with my mother at the camp.'

'The camp?' He saw the horrified pity on Helga's face. 'You are ... jüdisch?'

'No. I think ... I think the Germans just wanted Vati's hospital. And people to work for them and an easy way to steal their jewellery and valuables. There were Juden in the camp, but not many when I was there. Most had already been killed.' He hesitated, thinking of the boy who had helped him when he first came to the camp. Had he been jüdisch? 'You don't like Juden?'

'I don't think I have ever met any,' said Helga softly. 'But I knew a woman who knew a jüdische family. They were good

73

people, she said. Wonderful people. And yet she and all the others let the soldiers take them to the camp, and the people who had sheltered them as well. I used to think that maybe if any jüdische people escaped, I would help them. But they never came.'

He could think of nothing to say. But he was glad Helga had wanted to help the Juden.

—

Days turned into weeks, and even months. Johannes had lost track of dates much earlier, in that first journey into the ogre's belly in the cattle car, and the Schmidts had lost count too.

Soon Johannes was strong enough to go looking for food with Helga, but she refused to let him. 'You need to stay warm.' She shrugged. 'I have a warm coat and woollen stockings; you don't. Rest.'

At least he had proper clothes, not the rag of a nightgown from the camp. He felt guilty for resting, for being almost warm and almost fed, when Mutti and Vati might be ... But he would not think of 'might be'.

For now there was the barn, the hay, Frau Schmidt getting stronger every day too, and Hannes. He even found himself telling Frau Schmidt and Hannes the story of the cow that sat on the farmer's wife's lap, and then some of Sister Columba's stories. Helga smiled at him when he made them laugh.

At night he tried to pray for Sister Columba, for Mutti, for Vati, for Oma and Opa, for the Schmidts and himself and the whole world, except for Hitler and all who followed him. And the Russians.

But he couldn't pray at all. The words wouldn't come. Maybe he was infected with hate too, like the soldiers, and the guards at the camps.

Every day Helga scavenged among the ruins. She still limped, but it seemed it wasn't an injury from the Russians who had hurt her mother. Once she cut herself badly in the debris, but the cut healed cleanly. Every day she found more food, knowing instinctively where there were cellars or the ruins of attics where onions might be drying, or an old plum crop shrivelling into prunes. They ate the onions raw and the swedes she found too, for they did not dare light a fire, not that they had matches. Smoke or a flickering light might bring strangers — not just soldiers, but others who were homeless and desperate. Even those who did not want to hurt them, or steal their food, might want to share their shed — and more people would make it harder for them to hide.

Everyone was an enemy now.

Helga found another cheese and two giant sausages, hidden in a collapsing chimney where they had been smoking; and half a ham, in yet another chimney, which the owners must have been hacking back slice by slice, and which the rats had gnawed too, but only a little. She found turnips, and a whole box full of apples, which she carried back bucketful by bucketful in case the rats ate them before she could go back for them the next day.

There were no more blankets, but she found a sewing kit and sheets, which Frau Schmidt carefully folded so she could make summer shirts for Hannes and Johannes, and blouses for Helga, if summer ever came again.

Helga found books too, one of poetry, which they took turns reading aloud, '*Röslein, Röslein, Röslein rot …*' for the song of the words and because the poems were from another world, where there were roses and roast potatoes and fresh bread.

Each day they heard people on the road beyond the village, sometimes many, marching by for hours, sometimes a car and once what sounded like a convoy of trucks. But this village must have been away from the highways, for hours passed with no one even on that main road at all. It was as if they had been shifted sideways from the world of war, into a time of almost-peace. Only each day seemed real, as if the past and future were burned away.

Apart from Helga, they left the barn only to use the privy behind what had been a cottage. It was almost funny, how in the whole village the only structures standing were the privy, entirely untouched, still with the moon shape cut out of its door, and the hay shed, which must have been half falling down even before the bombs destroyed the house near it. Around them the world was black and white; white snow, and black where the cottages had burned after the bombs had fallen, staining even the stonework.

Johannes could breathe easily now, after these weeks of rest and food. At last Helga let him join her in her hunt through the ruins, while Hannes stayed to watch over Frau Schmidt, who still slept a great deal, fitfully, moaning in pain and nightmare.

It was fun, in a strange way. A true treasure hunt, where even a withered carrot was valuable. Within half an hour on the first night Johannes had a half-rotted marrow in his arms and three odd socks tied about his arm, as a way to carry them. Helga carried a leaky bucket they might use for washing, and a bag of barley that had probably been kept for seed, but which might still be eaten, if they could find a safe way to light a fire to cook it. It would be wonderful to have cooked food again.

'Do you think we could light a fire in one of the chimneys at night? No one would see the smoke then,' he asked as they walked back to the barn, the dawn sitting pink on the shattered horizon.

Helga considered. 'That's a good idea. We could try to catch the pigeons that roost in the barn to make soup. Pigeon soup is strengthening.'

'What about getting their feathers off? And their insides out?' Lottie had done that at home, so he knew it wasn't easy.

'I know how to.'

'How do you know so many things? Like plucking pigeons and where to find food?'

Helga shrugged. 'I lived on a farm for a while. Frau Leib, a farmer's wife, was our housekeeper. She showed me how to dry fruit and vegetables in the attic, roots in the cellar, hams in the chimney, how to cover cheese with wax. She could pluck and gut a pigeon in three minutes.' Helga smiled. 'She was very proud of that.'

'I thought you lived in Berlin?'

Helga hesitated. 'It was a holiday on the farm.'

Something was wrong. But he couldn't think what it might be. He said instead, 'I have no identity papers.' All his life he'd had to show papers to travel anywhere. 'Do you have yours?'

Helga nodded. 'Mutti has them.'

'Hannes said you had a special pass that let you on the train.' It was just an idle comment, to pass the time. But she flinched, as if he had hit her.

'I found it. It must have belonged to a Nazi official's family.'

'Where is it?'

'I tore it up after we left the train.'

'Why?' It sounded too useful to discard.

'I might have got into trouble if anyone found I had it.'

It sounded like the truth, but something more too. Again there were questions he didn't know how to frame. Instead he said what was deepest in his heart: 'Do you think I will find Mutti again? And Vati?'

Helga considered. He liked that she did not just reassure him and say, 'Of course,' or shrug and say, 'Who can tell?' or even, 'No — you escaped, but the others will have been killed.'

At last she said, 'I think you will. There's a good chance anyway.'
'Why?'

'Because *you* escaped.' She saw he didn't understand. 'You are clever. Strong. Even when you were sick, you hid. You found a way out of the camp. And you are *nice*.' She said it without smiling, as if being nice was just like being short or tall. 'People like to help nice people. That is why those people helped you, even if they put you off the train later.'

'Is that why you helped me? But you couldn't know I was nice then.' He was glad she thought he was a nice person.

'I helped you because …' Her face twisted in anguish. 'Because I must,' she said eventually. 'I … I can't say more. But I have to help people. I must.'

'Why does my being nice mean Mutti and Vati might be alive?'

She relaxed. 'Because you must be like your parents. They will be clever and brave and nice too. They must be nice, if they are both doctors. People who help people. You are lucky, to have parents like that.'

'Aren't your parents nice?' Frau Schmidt was ill and confused, but when she made sense, she seemed gentle and kind.

'Of course!'

'You really think Mutti and Vati might escape?'

'I really do. And people might help them, as they will help other people. That gives them a better chance of survival.'

'I see.' For the first time he almost felt hope, among the hate.

A siren screamed a long way off, a wail that ripped the air even at this distance. Hannes peered out of the barn and waved frantically at them when he saw they were coming back. 'Bombers!' he cried.

And then they heard them: a vast eruption of the air. Johannes looked up, wonderingly, as half the sky turned grey with planes.

Helga grabbed his arm. 'We have to get to a cellar,' she said desperately as Frau Schmidt looked out of the barn door, frightened, then tried to smile reassuringly at Hannes.

'The planes won't waste their bombs on this village.' Johannes hoped that was true. 'It's been bombed already. They'll be looking for barracks, factories, soldiers. We are as safe here as anywhere. Come on!'

He dived back into the barn as Helga said, 'I think —'

The world exploded. The barn shook. The air shivered, shimmered. Impossible to hear, or even stand. Johannes crawled into the straw and covered his ears.

The noise went on and on until at last he managed to distinguish many smaller sounds: the dull thuds when bombs hit, the earthquake of sound and vibration of explosions, the rattle of machine-gun fire. Instinctively, they drew together, Frau Schmidt's arms around Hannes and Helga, Helga's around Frau Schmidt and Johannes. On and on and on ...

And then the noise was sliced away.

Almost. Guns still rattled. Vague booms burped like a vast cow with indigestion. But at least the air and ground were still.

'We are alive,' said Frau Schmidt softly.

Johannes nodded. But still they stayed there, not moving, till darkness came, and then they slept, the blankets over them all, in a huddle of comfort that was almost warm.

Chapter 19

JOHANNES
GERMANY, MARCH? APRIL? 1945

The jeeps came the next day.

Helga had crept out, in the pre-dawn light, to fetch water. Johannes listened when he heard the first engine on the road, hoping she had hidden in time. But she came running back, the bucket forgotten. 'English! There were jeeps on the road with people speaking English!'

'You speak English?' He had never met anyone else his own age who spoke English.

'Yes,' said Helga as Hannes and Frau Schmidt shook their heads. 'But don't you see?' she cried. 'They must be American or English. We can ask them which way to go, to keep away from the Russians.'

'Maybe the war is over,' said Frau Schmidt hopefully.

Helga nodded. 'I'll wait by the road. Don't worry — I'll hide if it is a Russian vehicle, or German.'

Johannes did not know how she knew one side's vehicles from another's. All children were taught at school which were enemy planes, and which were German, but now the enemies had changed places.

'We should all stay together,' said Frau Schmidt.

Helga shook her head. She met Frau Schmidt's eyes. 'You must keep Hannes and Johannes safe. I speak English.'

'So do I …' said Johannes.

'There is no need for two of us.'

So Helga too knew it was a risk. Soldiers were soldiers. How did they know the English or American soldiers would not behave just as the Russians had? Surely their countries too had been hurt in this war.

'I will go. Not you,' Johannes insisted.

Helga looked hard at him. 'Please,' she said to Johannes. 'Please let me do this. It is important.'

He saw her face, her pleading face, blotched by its red birthmark. Why did doing this for them matter to her so much? He could not argue with her and her quiet determination.

Helga slipped out the door. They waited, not speaking, listening to every squeak of the mice, every clatter of far-off guns. At last they heard an engine, and another.

The engines stopped.

They have seen her, thought Johannes. He clenched his fists and realised he was sweating with the tension. He waited for the snicker of a revolver, or for Helga to scream.

But Helga would not scream. No matter what they did to her, she would stay quiet, so that the others would not run out to help her and be caught too.

The engines started again. The sound drifted into the distance.

Johannes counted under his breath. When he got to ten, he would go and find her.

'Look!' Helga ran into the barn. She held up four blocks of chocolate and two packets of cigarettes.

'Chocolate!' yelled Hannes.

'But we don't smoke,' said Johannes.

Frau Schmidt laughed. Johannes realised he had never heard her laugh so easily before. 'But others do. When you smoke, you *have* to smoke, so people will swap food for cigarettes. Helga, were they English?'

'American! They said there is a women's camp across the forest. That way.' She pointed. 'They said if we walk now, we should get there by dark. It was a German work camp — a true work camp, not a concentration camp — but the Americans have taken it over now. They said we'll be safe there.'

'The war is over?' demanded Frau Schmidt.

Helga shook her head. 'No. The Russian soldiers are nearby, and German troops too. We must be careful, the Americans said. But they told me we'd be safer at the camp than here, with food and beds,' she glanced at Frau Schmidt, 'and doctors.'

Doctors! Maybe Mutti and Vati had been directed to the camp too.

He looked at the chocolate. He could taste its smoothness, richness already. 'Should we eat that now?'

'One block now,' said Frau Schmidt. She was taking charge — maybe she knew she had enough strength to be the mama again, now safety was so close. 'We finish the cheese, the other food, before we go. The chocolate is light to carry.'

It felt strange, forcing himself to eat so much. Two raw onions, a raw swede, the marrow, seven shrivelled apples, a handful of cheese, four mouthfuls of ham, on top of the chocolate. He felt slightly sick.

It was hard to leave the barn. It had sheltered them so well: the first place he had been safe since home. He stopped in the doorway as a single plane flew past, and then more. American planes, high in the air.

'Heading for Berlin,' said Frau Schmidt.

'Maybe they'll kill Hitler.' Johannes almost didn't recognise his own voice, so thick with hatred. 'I hope they crush him. Rip him into pieces. I hope they kill them all!'

He meant the Germans. Though of course Helga, Hannes and Frau Schmidt were Germans too.

'Hitler is already dead,' said Helga flatly. 'He killed himself. The Americans told me.'

Frau Schmidt stared at her. 'Why didn't you tell us? This is wonderful!'

'I hope he's very dead,' said Johannes. 'I hope it hurt and hurt.'

Helga wobbled, then sat down hard, in the doorway of the barn. 'Hitler is dead,' she whispered. 'Hitler is dead.'

'Yes,' said Frau Schmidt gently, helping her up. 'The monster is dead. Soon the war will be over. Soon we will be safe.' She put her arm around Helga. 'You have cared for us so wonderfully. Now let us care for you.'

They gathered their scavenged possessions into bundles, and walked towards the forest.

Chapter 20

JOHANNES
GERMANY, MAY 1945

The snow had vanished into the earth and air. Branches cracked underfoot. The trees were too sparse to hide them from soldiers, but it was still safer than walking along the road, where trucks and tanks would certainly find them.

'Which way?' asked Frau Schmidt.

Helga hesitated, then pointed. 'That way,' she said.

They walked. As the sun rose higher, they stopped and ate chocolate.

'We should have brought a bucket of water,' said Frau Schmidt.

Johannes remembered the thirst in the cattle car and shuddered, but soon after they began to walk again a spring bubbled up, cold and sweet.

They drank. They walked. Frau Schmidt lagged now, sweat on her face, although the day was cold. Whatever was wrong with her had not yet healed.

Shots. Johannes turned and saw far-off figures floundering

among the trees, too distant to distinguish. The four of them flung themselves onto the ground, lying still, even without Frau Schmidt's whisper to be quiet.

A woman screamed, and then another — perhaps the same woman. Two more shots.

They waited, still as the fallen branches. At last Johannes peered up.

The forest seemed quiet.

They walked more cautiously now. The sun sank into a red ball, bouncing on the horizon. Shadows purpled, gathered the whole forest in. Then they saw the light. A big light, or many lights.

'There!' cried Frau Schmidt triumphantly.

Johannes hesitated. What if they had come the wrong way? What if it was a prison camp? For the others a camp meant safety, but for him …

'Come,' urged Frau Schmidt. She began to run, stumbling through the trees towards the light. The others followed her.

A clearing, the trees felled. Lights. Barbed-wire fences. A barbed-wire gate. But this barbed wire was only single strands wound around posts. It looked as if it were meant to keep people out, not people in. Perhaps they really were safe …

A shot cracked out from behind them. Someone yelled, in German.

Hannes slumped to the ground.

Frau Schmidt screamed. She flung herself on her son, held him in her arms. Helga made no sound, but hugged them both, as if to take any other shot into her body, not theirs. Johannes froze, trying to work out what to do.

More yells, in English this time. Men in strange uniforms ran from the gate and fired past them towards the trees. One ran to them. 'You okay?' he asked.

English. He was English. No, American. Johannes glanced back at the trees, but whoever had shot at them was gone.

And Hannes was dead.

Chapter 21

JOHANNES
GERMANY, MAY 1945

They had three bunks, together, in a corridor, but they were at the end, almost as if they had a room of their own. Buckets of water to wash in — cold but clean, and even a shrivelled piece of soap and threadbare towels. Pillows, sheets, quilts; bread and ersatz coffee for breakfast; bread and cocoa and cheese for supper; but a hot meal in the dining room each midday, of tinned meat and vegetables all stewed up — not tasting particularly good, but filling.

Frau Schmidt did not leave her bed, so Helga and Johannes took turns staying with her, the other bringing two bowls of stew back, making sure Frau Schmidt ate.

'She's ill,' said Helga softly as at last Frau Schmidt fell into a mumbling sleep. 'It isn't just the grief over Hannes. She has lost everything. Her home, her children, her husband ...'

'Children? You had another brother or sister who died?'

'What? No. I mean ... other children. Cousins. Friends. So many children have been lost in this war. All the families we knew.'

Johannes nodded.

More people arrived each day, men as well as women, whole families, their houses and villages destroyed by bombs or taken by the still-fighting armies. Sometimes the people looked battered, bloodied and in shock, as if their lives had vanished suddenly. Others wore the wide-eyed stare of concentration camps, those who knew that death had been long planned for them, but had survived. Most of these were brought from hospitals, or from the houses where the owners had been paid — or forced, unwillingly or even cruelly — to care for them, for there were not hospitals enough for all who needed them. Their bodies had recovered, at least enough to travel. Unlike the other refugees, they had long known their past lives were gone forever.

Every day he hoped Mutti might arrive, or Vati, or someone who knew them. But no one had heard of a Dr Wolcheki. There were no doctors in the camp, nor any nurses, so there was no one they could ask to help Frau Schmidt, despite what the Americans had told Helga.

Even if there had been, Johannes knew enough about medicine to know that any internal injuries from the Russian soldiers were probably infected, and would have been so for a long time. There was nothing that could be done for infections like that, except for rest and care, or sulpha drugs. Even back before the ogre there had been few such drugs in Vati's hospital, and only for families of members of the Nazi Party. There would be no chance of finding sulpha drugs for Frau Schmidt in a camp like this.

The camp had no radio for the inmates, nor did the Americans provide more than protection and food, but the newcomers brought news from the outside world: Russians here, Allies there. The war battered on, but at least it did not batter here.

At night the camp gate was shut, but only to keep roving soldiers out. Most of the German army, it seemed, had deserted, and was combing the countryside for pillage or food. But still the planes flew overhead; still the thunderstorms were the sounds of war, not rain.

Green fuzzed the trees, for spring. A patch of white bloomed — snowdrops, not snow. The air turned sweet with the scent of growing things. Helga and Johannes helped Frau Schmidt out into the sunlight.

'My father says sunlight is good for you,' said Johannes. 'All the patients at his TB hospital sat in the sunlight twice a day, and in the glassed-in area when it rained or was too cold.'

Frau Schmidt smiled vaguely. She walked, hesitantly, one hand holding Johannes's, the other Helga's. Helga hardly left her side these days.

Johannes spread a blanket on the ground. They sat and watched more stragglers arrive: two elderly women, each carrying a baby; a mother and father and two children, younger than Johannes, but even the children carried two suitcases each, all that was left, he thought, of their old lives. An American truck filled with grey men in grey rags, who looked like they had been prisoners. The soldiers helped the men down. Some could hardly walk. But they were all smiling.

Smiling?

One of the men stopped inside the gate. Tears ran down his cheeks, even as he smiled. He came no further in, just stood and yelled, 'It's over! The war is over!'

'What?' Frau Schmidt struggled to her feet. All around them others were shrieking too.

'It's over? Is it really over?'

Johannes ran to the fence. 'Is it really finished?' he asked the American soldier, a black man, the first black man Johannes had ever met.

The soldier's voice was deep and kind. 'Yes, kid, it's over.'

What was a kid? 'Thank you,' said Johannes politely.

'Here.' The soldier handed him two packets of chewing gum.

'Thank you,' said Johannes again, and he shoved them in his pocket. Chewing gum could be traded, just like cigarettes.

Someone had brought out a violin, and women danced, women with white faces dancing with men with hollow eyes.

'It's over,' whispered Frau Schmidt. 'Mein Gott, at last. The war is over.'

'Yes,' said Helga, not rejoicing like the others, her voice empty. 'It is over.'

Chapter 22

JOHANNES
GERMANY, 1945

Nothing changed, except the faces. Many people left to see whether there was anything left of their homes, to try to find relatives or friends or shelter. As many came for refuge. American trucks brought soldiers, food. Planes still criss-crossed the sky.

Pieces of paper grew like butterflies on the doors of the dining room, small almost-poems. 'Does anyone know Frau Gruner? I am her daughter.' Or just a name, Konrad Freuden, and a question mark. Sometimes a reply was scribbled on the bottom of the note. 'My friend says she worked in the uniform factory and was safe when last seen in September.' But mostly people studied them, in hope, then shook their heads and walked away.

At last the mealtime gossip said that there were new camps being set up under British or American control in the western section of Germany. No formal announcement was made, but now the trucks that had brought the soldiers and ex-prisoners took people away instead, to the new camps, as many volunteers as could fit in every truck.

Every person must go home. If you could not go home because the Russians had occupied your homeland, as they occupied Poland, and the part of Berlin where the Schmidts had lived, you were 'a displaced person'. Displaced persons would have new camps, created especially for them.

Displaced, thought Johannes. It was a good word. He had been displaced from the real world, swallowed.

'We need to go to one of the new camps,' said Johannes. 'The closest one.'

Helga looked at him in surprise. 'Why?'

'Why not? No new people are being brought here, but maybe my parents or your father are in one of the new camps. Maybe there will be records of who is where, so people can find each other. If we are put on a list, my parents or your father might even find us too.'

Maybe, somewhere, his life still waited for him, his real life. Maybe even with the Russians in charge, they could go home. Helga and Frau Schmidt could come with them, share their big house ...

Helga shook her head. 'The journey might be bad for Frau Schmidt. We don't know what it is like in the new camps. Here we have beds, enough food ...'

'They say there are beds and food in the other camps too.' Johannes had asked the black soldier. He had been kind and given him two more packets of chewing gum and three blocks of chocolate. Johannes did not think the soldier would lie about the displaced persons camps. And he and Helga and Frau Schmidt *were* displaced. Perhaps such a camp was the best place to be 'placed' again.

'Please come,' he said. He *had* to find Mutti and Vati, but he knew he could not leave Helga and Frau Schmidt behind either.

'All right,' said Helga.

The black soldier helped Frau Schmidt up into the truck. He did not seem to see the camp's pillows Helga was carrying under their bundles of clothes so that Frau Schmidt would be more comfortable on the journey. 'Here, kids,' he handed Johannes another block of chocolate, and one to Helga too, 'you look after yourselves, and your mom too. Okay?'

'Okay' meant yes. 'Okay,' said Johannes. His mind was too full of other things to explain to the soldier that he was not related to Helga or Frau Schmidt.

The truck drove. Villages, as perfect as if they had been frozen all the war and thawed out, still perfect when it ended. Piles of rubble that had been villages, but where people now peeped out of cellars that were the only shelter left. Forests, sometimes standing like a wall of Christmas trees, sometimes shattered into matchsticks by the bombs. A train station, where women waited, holding placards with the names of their husbands, fathers, sons, even those not 'displaced', desperate for news of those who might be dead, or lost, or miraculously found.

And then the camp.

It was a camp. Exactly that. Barbed wire, the kind to keep people out, not in. Barracks, and not new ones. No one said what it had been used for before, nor did Johannes ask. He did not want to know if the people who had been here before had been the killers, or the killed.

He and Helga helped Frau Schmidt out of the truck. They stood in line, carrying their bundles, while guards stood next to two soldiers at two desks, checking papers.

At last they reached a desk. 'Papers,' said the soldier, not looking up. Frau Schmidt held out hers and Helga's. The soldier nodded. 'What about your son's?'

'My name is Johannes Wolcheki,' said Johannes. 'I am not part of their family.' And yet they were a family, he realised, bound together by so much.

Would he be sent away, into the forest, because he had no papers? Would he not exist? Perhaps he should have asked Frau Schmidt if he could have used Hannes's papers. But he couldn't rob the dead boy of the only thing of his that was left, and, in any case, he needed to be himself here, in case his parents were searching for him.

But the soldier simply nodded, as if he was used to people with no papers. He began to scribble on a form. 'Name? Date of birth? Parents?' he asked in German.

Helga waited, supporting Frau Schmidt, while Johannes answered all the questions, was given papers — his own papers, with the big letters 'DP' stamped on them.

Displaced person. But he *was* a person now, at last a legal person once again.

'Please,' said Helga to the soldier. 'Is there a hospital? Mutti needs help.'

'Over there.' The soldier waved vaguely. 'Next!'

They stumbled to the furthest barracks building, grey, like every set of barracks sitting on the grassless ground. Johannes opened the door.

Beds, double bunks, all crammed in long lines, with just enough space to walk between the rows. The strong stench of disinfectant.

And then a voice.

'Johannes!'

It was Nurse Stöhlich.

94

Chapter 23

JOHANNES
GERMANY, 1945

'Oh, Johannes. Johannes!' He found himself being hugged, then kissed.

He broke away. 'Mutti?' Please, he thought, *please*.

'She is here.'

'In this camp?'

'In this hospital. But she will be well. She will certainly be well, now you are here. And Johannes ...'

But he didn't wait. He ran up and down the aisles. 'Mutti!' he yelled. 'Mutti!' And there she was, trying to leave her bunk, her face white, white as her nightdress, reaching for him, her arms around him. 'Mutti. Mutti.'

'Johannes. It is all right. It is all right now. Here, let me look at you. Are you well? You have been *eating*!'

'Mutti, Mutti ...' He stopped as a doctor approached. A doctor in a white coat, with a stethoscope dangling around his neck.

'Johannes,' said the doctor softly.

'Vati,' said Johannes.

—✲◉

Nurse Stöhlich organised it all. Moved the patient from the bed next to Mutti's so that Frau Schmidt could take her place. Found Frau Schmidt a nightdress, covered her with a sheet and quilt, brought bread and margarine and cocoa, which Johannes and Helga ate and drank while Nurse Stöhlich coaxed Frau Schmidt to eat too and Mutti, and Vati as well. 'Because you doctors always forget to eat, you are so busy,' said Nurse Stöhlich.

At last Vati said that they must go. 'Just to the other barracks for now.'

'I don't want to —' said Johannes and Helga together.

But Vati was a doctor now, as well as a father. 'The people in the hospital need to rest. You may visit again tonight.' And then, to Helga, 'I think your mother will recover. Truly I do.'

'You have sulpha here?' asked Johannes.

Vati smiled. He looked younger than when they'd arrived. The smile grew as if it would not leave his face. 'My little doctor. No, no sulpha. But with care Frau Schmidt should not get worse.' He means that if she has survived till now, she will keep living, thought Johannes, and saw that Helga understood as well.

'And Mutti?' he asked softly, but Mutti heard.

'I am quite capable of diagnosing myself! No infection, thanks to a good nurse, clean bandages and much carbolic. I am nearly better.'

'Nearly is not healed,' said Vati, still with his smile spread across his face. 'You will stay here till you are completely well again.'

'Yes, doctor,' said Mutti, which was a game they used to play, each calling the other 'doctor'.

Johannes felt Vati's smile on his own face too. 'Vati ... can we go home again, when Mutti is better?'

The smile dimmed. 'We will go home,' said Vati quietly. 'But it will be a new home. The hospital, the house, they are in the Russian zone. We could go back.' He shrugged. 'But the hospital was bombed, and the house too, as it was being used as German headquarters. There is nothing to go back to, except to Russian rule. We have had enough dictators, enough foreigners disposing of our lives. But we will make a new home. I promise, Johannes.' He bent and hugged him again. 'We have come so far. We can keep going. Now you go with your friend, and find a bed and supper — then you can come back and visit.' The smile came again. 'But for an hour only, like a proper visitor.'

They left.

~✻❀✻~

Bunk beds in dormitories. 'She is my sister,' lied Johannes when they tried to put him in the men's dormitory and Helga in the women's, hoping no one would ask to see their ID papers. At last they put them both in the dormitory for families, each family's space separated by hanging blankets.

So many strangers, milling around, arguing about where the Russians were, or what villages were left, others crying or standing silent, children wailing or sitting, staring at the wall. More fluttering hearts on paper, crying silently for news. Too many people, too much emotion, everything confused and confusing.

Except for Mutti and Vati, over in the hospital. Except for the warmth of Helga's hand. The world might twist and swirl, and gargoyles might leer at night, and the sounds of screaming and shooting return. But now there was a small ball of warmth to hold onto, a ball of light, as well as the flame of hate, to keep him warm through the night.

In the end he and Helga were not just hospital visitors. There were too many patients and too few nurses. When Nurse Stöhlich saw Helga carrying Frau Schmidt's chamberpot, she asked her softly if she would mind helping empty some others as well. Johannes joined her, carrying the stinking contents, emptying them in the trench behind the barracks, washing them, and then washing their hands thoroughly too.

'If we do not keep our hands clean, we may get infections from the patients through their chamberpots,' said Johannes.

'Yes, of course,' said Helga. But she didn't smile. She hadn't smiled since Hannes's death.

The camp was an international one, whatever that meant, but English people ran it. The food was not as good or plentiful as at the American camp, just cocoa and bread and margarine for breakfast, a soup of vegetables at lunch, mostly turnip or swede, more bread and margarine and cocoa for their supper. But Red Cross parcels came through, and although the workers in the office took some of the contents to sell on the black market, chocolate and dry biscuits, dried fruit and even cakes were still distributed, irregularly but often enough to survive on the scant camp food. There were also cigarettes, two packets in each parcel, which Helga and Johannes traded for more food.

The food was better in the hospital, meat sometimes in the stew, and always potatoes, and sometimes porridge made from rolled oats from the Red Cross parcels. As Johannes and Helga helped there, Nurse Stöhlich said they should share the patients' food as well.

It was a well-run hospital. Only once did Johannes see Vati angry, when he found one of the nurses had failed to feed a woman in the far corner of the ward.

'Why?' demanded Vati, glaring at the nurse. 'She says she has not been fed for two days! How can you do this?'

'She is jüdisch,' spat out the nurse.

Johannes thought: Hitler is dead, but he is still alive in these people. And hatred flared again in a small bright core inside him.

Vati looked at the nurse, then at the ill woman, thin and trembling on the bed. 'You will leave the hospital and not come back.'

'But I am a nurse! I have my papers!'

'I will tear your papers into little shreds and tell them you are a fraud if you do not go. Now!'

The nurse spat towards the woman. 'Juden,' she hissed, one last time.

'Helga, will you feed …' Vati bent to hear the woman's name; she whispered and he said, 'Frau Liebermann? Helga, will you please give her a meal?'

And Helga smiled, her first smile in so long, and took the woman's hand. 'It will make me very happy,' she said. And Johannes saw it was the truth.

A strange girl. And yet he loved her anyway.

Chapter 24

'Frau Marks! Does anyone know a Frau Marks?' An English soldier moved through the bunks in the barracks, a shabby German translator at his side. 'Wer kennt eine Frau Marks?'

No one answered. Those who had survived knew that to give someone's name might see them hauled into the night. 'She might be known as Fräulein Stöhlich,' the translator added.

Johannes peered around the blanket that divided their space from the other families'. The camp's outside lights stayed on all night, but the dining room lights were turned off after supper, so the only place to talk or play cards after dark was in the dormitories. Nurse Stöhlich! He glanced at Helga. She looked at the English soldier, at the translator in his faded and frayed overcoat, then nodded almost imperceptibly.

Yes, thought Johannes. This was an Englishman. And Nurse Stöhlich's sister-in-law was English, because she had sent her son to England. He stood. 'I can show you,' he said carefully in English.

The Englishman looked at him. A major, an important man. 'You speak English?'

'A little.'

'She is here? You can take me to her?'

Johannes nodded. He could have told him she'd be in the hospital, or in the room she shared with other nurses nearby. But he wanted to be there when this important man was shown who she was in case this meant trouble for her. If it did, he could help her run and hide. Among the bunks, maybe, then out into the forest. He could smuggle her out chocolate and cigarettes so she could trade them for food.

He could not think what Nurse Stöhlich might have done that would get her into trouble. But what you did in this world was less important than where you were or what you were, like being jüdisch.

'Ich komme auch,' said Helga. I'm coming too.

Good, thought Johannes. If they needed a diversion, to get Nurse Stöhlich to safety, Helga would help, and Mutti and Vati too, if they were on duty, for his mother was well enough to work a little now.

Through the bunks, outside into the cold air — for although it was summer now, summer seemed as confused as everyone in this strange land. It was still a land of war, even though the war had ceased.

Into the hospital. The other staff were used to Johannes and Helga now. 'Why do you need to find her?' Johannes asked just as Nurse Stöhlich came around the bunks and saw them.

'Is everything all right?' she asked.

'No,' said Johannes. 'The English soldier is looking for you.'

'For me?' Nurse Stöhlich looked at the soldier and the translator. 'Good evening,' she said in English. 'I am Nurse Stöhlich.'

The major stared at her. Suddenly Johannes saw what the English soldier saw: a woman like a skeleton, with a little hair growing in tufts, her hands red and swollen from small infections from dealing every day with wounds that oozed pus, with washing them over and over again in cold water and carbolic soap, the only disinfectant that they had. Her lips caved in over her empty mouth, where once there had been teeth.

'Are you Mrs Marks?' he asked, in English.

'Yes.' Nurse Stöhlich ... or Frau Marks ... seemed to have lost her breath. 'Why do you want me?'

The soldier stared. He had expected to see a young woman, Johannes realised. How old was Frau Marks? Thirty-five?

She looked eighty. All the women in the camp, even Mutti and Frau Schmidt, looked old, older than crumpled ancient castles.

'You have a sister-in-law in England?'

'Miriam! Georg ... is Georg alive? Are they both alive?'

'Yes,' said the major gently. 'They are both alive. Your sister-in-law is a woman of great determination, Mrs Marks. And influence. She has arranged for you to go to England.' He cleared his throat. 'Do you have any identification? Papers? A passport?'

No! thought Johannes. Of course she didn't have any, except the ones that said DP and the names she had given to be allowed in here. No one who had been in the extermination camps had proper papers! Didn't the major know that? Would he leave Frau Marks here because she had no proper papers?

'I have my passport,' said Frau Marks carefully. 'My English passport and my German one. They are hidden in the hospital where I was taken prisoner. The Germans occupied it, but I don't think they would have found my papers. It is about an hour's drive from here, if someone could take me?'

She knows where we are, thought Johannes. He realised he had never thought about where they might be on the map he had known at school. In the belly of the ogre you did not think of maps.

'My driver will take you,' said the major, then stopped as Frau Marks began to cry. She held out her arms to Johannes and to Helga.

'Georg,' whispered Frau Marks as she hugged them. 'I will see Georg.'

The papers must have still been in the hiding place, for the next morning Frau Marks was gone, taken away in an ambulance, Mutti said, one ambulance just for her, as if she were a soldier. Johannes had never thought that Nurse Stöhlich was sick. She cared for the sick! But the English major must have thought so.

The major came to see Johannes one more time. He brought a loaf of bread and a tin of jam — opened, in case they had no can opener — and a piece of cheese. Johannes thought it must be the major's own food, for the English had no big warehouses where food could be bought, like the Americans had.

The major sat with them, while he and Helga and Frau Schmidt ate the bread slowly, and then the cheese, and spoon after spoon of jam. You did not leave food uneaten in the camp, unless it was small enough to put under your pillow wrapped in a corner of the sheet and tied to your wrist so no one could steal it in the night.

The major stood when Mutti came in. He handed her a small twist of paper. 'From Mrs Marks,' he said. 'She told me how you saved each other's lives. She asked if I could help you. Mrs Wolcheki, I wish I could —'

'Dr Wolcheki,' said Mutti.

'Dr Wolcheki. But Britain is only taking single men, not families. There is nothing I can do.'

'Thank you,' said Mutti politely.

'Good luck, young man,' said the major. He nodded to the Schmidts, who said 'Guten Tag' politely back, though Frau Schmidt had not understood the talk in English. Johannes saw pity in the major's eyes, and anger and guilt, and all the feelings of a good man who had seen too much and could do nothing, or not more than he had done.

He left.

Later, when it was dark, Mutti opened the paper. It was a ring, too big for her thin fingers, with a red stone, like blood. She wrapped it in cloth and hung it around her neck to hide it.

Chapter 25

JOHANNES
GERMANY, 1945–1946

People came, frightened people, lugging all the debris of their lives that they could carry. People left, as the effects of war ebbed, for even after Germany surrendered it took months to capture the bands of soldiers, to stop them looting, killing, spreading the disease of war even though peace had been declared.

Slowly, those who had homes, or land where new homes might be built, or friends or relatives to take them in, left. The food grew worse — Germany had had little chance to grow food, nor had the English had time to grow enough food even for themselves and fight a war too, much less enough to send to Germany to feed displaced people.

But Red Cross parcels continued to arrive from countries across the world: tinned meat, chocolate, more cigarettes to trade. The parcels meant they didn't starve. But every day was spent thinking about food, wondering if they would be weak with hunger by the night, or if a parcel might arrive, or someone might trade some jewellery with the farmers outside the camp.

Frau Schmidt joined them now, sharing Helga's bunk. Helga no longer helped at the hospital, for Frau Schmidt needed her, holding her hand, or listening to stories of when she and Hannes were young.

Helga never joined in the stories, never said, 'I remember when ...' It was as if Frau Schmidt was reading the memories from a book, as she lay on her bunk, her eyes closed, looking at the past, speaking about Helga as if she were not there. '... and then Hannes and Helga caught tadpoles in the lake. Those tadpoles! Hannes kept them in a jar in the kitchen and one morning — plop! A frog jumped into the milk. And Helga said ...'

'What did I say, Mutti?'

'You said, "Other frogs live in the water. We have Berlin's only milk frogs."' She began to weep again.

Vati and Mutti had a small room at the end of the hospital that they shared with two nurses, taking turns, two on duty and two asleep. They worked long hours, for there were many sick people and with no sulpha drugs or the new medicine called penicillin there was no quick way to make them well. So Johannes stayed with the Schmidts, carrying their midday meals in to eat in their own tiny world behind the blanket.

Then one day he arrived with the tray to find the blanket pushed aside. A man sat on Frau Schmidt's bunk, a strange man, holding her hands.

Not a doctor in a white coat. A thief maybe, after the cigarettes, chocolate and chewing gum they kept under Frau Schmidt's pillow? But then he saw that Helga stood there, her face carefully blank. Helga would not just stand there and let a thief take the precious things they had to trade.

'Helga?' he asked.

But the man answered. He held out his hand for Johannes to shake. 'I am Herr Schmidt,' he said.

Chapter 26

Herr Schmidt shared Frau Schmidt's bunk now, and Helga had another. It felt strange at first, having Herr Schmidt there, added to their 'family'. Even Helga seemed to find it strange. But Herr Schmidt had been away for most of the war, an engineer, working for the army. How old had she been when he left home? Six? Seven?

No wonder it felt strange for her to have a father, and strange for him to have a daughter her age too.

'Thank you for caring for my family,' he said quietly to Johannes, that first day, when Frau Schmidt was sleeping again. For the first time since Hannes's death there was a faint smile on her face. 'And thank you, Helga. Without you, I would have no family at all.' Johannes saw tears in his eyes as he added, 'All across the world now men are coming home to find they have no home, and have no family either. But I have a family. I have a wife. I have a daughter.'

He smiled at Helga as he said, 'I am a lucky man, to have a wife and a daughter. And one day, I promise, we will have a home again.'

A nurse at the hospital one day said there were twenty million displaced persons in Europe now. Twenty *million*! That was almost a quarter of all the people on the continent! So many that no one bothered to say the whole words now. They were just DPs.

Too many places had been destroyed. People must remain displaced till more houses were built, more crops sown, more order established in shattered lands.

Mutti and Vati worked, though they received no pay at first, as the foreign doctors did. Finally someone noticed that the hospital's main doctors were DPs, and they too were given envelopes of money every week.

But the German money bought little food; nor was there much food to buy. Frau Schmidt took out the sheets from the bombed-out village — so long ago that seemed — and made Helga a blouse and new skirts and Johannes a new shirt. Her sewing was so fine that women and men came to her with ragged clothes, asking her to mend them, to turn two old dresses into one that looked almost new.

Frau Schmidt sat in the sunlight, as the breeze blew through the leaves, and showed Helga how to hem and embroider. The sewing earned them cigarettes and chewing gum and cans of corned beef, more valuable than paper currency.

But, most of all, the work made Frau Schmidt live in the world again, talking to people about whether they'd like long sleeves or short, and what shape pocket, coming to the dining room to eat, and even to the concerts the inmates put on. There had been violins and flutes and even a banjo and a trombone in the ragged bundles carried to the camp.

Vati tried to organise a school, though no one else, it seemed, thought that important, and he could not run a school and the hospital as well. But an old man who had been a professor of mathematics before he was sent to a labour camp agreed to teach Johannes and Helga in return for one cigarette a day. He sat with them out in the sun. Paper was scarce, and ink and pencils even more so, but the professor filled a box with sand and found three straight sticks in the forest.

'This is what the ancient Greeks used to teach their students,' he said. 'If it was good enough for Plato's school, it will do for us.'

Soon other people joined them: a woman who had worked for an English firm before the war gave them English lessons, not for cigarettes, but for something to do. A sailor taught them geography, which was really stories about all the ports he'd seen. 'But not about the women,' said Frau Schmidt sternly. She was much better now.

A researcher who had a degree in physics; a chemist; and Herr Schmidt taught them geometry and the basics of engineering. It was a strange school. But, remembering his lessons of what was now over a year earlier, Johannes thought he learned far more there in the camp than he had sitting at a desk. No dull exercises in dull books. Just questions, conversations in the sunshine. Helga drank in knowledge too. It was as if they learned hand in hand, as they had been so often since the barn. But this was excitement as the world beyond the camp unfolded in the words of their teachers. He had never had a partner in learning before, one with a mind as sharp and enquiring as his own.

After a month, Helga shyly asked Mutti and Vati if they might teach at the 'school' too. And so lessons in anatomy were added, the bones of the foot outlined in their sand 'textbook', or the different areas of the brain, and what various viruses looked like — or would, if they were vastly bigger, and drawn with a finger or a stick.

The school moved inside to the Schmidts' bunk when autumn came. Christmas — snow, decorations made from scraps of coloured paper, and even canned ham served for midday dinner, with potatoes and peas. Vati and Mutti gave Johannes and Helga books they had traded for cigarettes from the Red Cross parcels; Helga gave each of them a hemmed handkerchief; the Schmidts gave Mutti and Helga blouses made from patchwork pieces of cloth and Johannes a shirt that was new, even if the blue cloth was faded, and he had last seen it in a woman's skirt. Johannes gave everyone notebooks he had made from brown wrapping paper.

The New Year came, with more snow. The men took it in turns to hunt for fuel in the forest, but there was little to be had, for so many others had looked for fallen wood too, and no one had cut timber for over a year, so none was dry enough to burn. The barracks grew cold again, the stoves only lit at night. They wore all their clothes all of the time, and were still cold.

That was when Herr Schmidt sat on his bunk with Frau Schmidt and Helga and Johannes one night and said, 'I must become a single man.'

'No,' said Frau Schmidt faintly. 'Please ...'

He took her hand. 'I must. It is the only way to get a home for us. The English, the Americans and the Canadians are only taking single men. I have my engineering papers — I am sure one of those countries will take me. If I go as a single man, then one day soon, surely, they will change this stupid rule and allow families to those countries too. I can send for you. And, in the meantime, I can send you money.'

Money they could exchange for better food. For fabric, for Frau Schmidt to make into clothes to sell. For books, for Helga — and Johannes — to study.

Frau Schmidt was very quiet. She took Helga's hand and held it tightly. And then she said, 'Yes. You should go. Go to America, with all its food. And when you can, send for us.'

Helga put her arms around her mother, and kissed her cheek. 'I will take care of you,' she said softly.

'You always do,' said Frau Schmidt, and she managed to smile at her daughter and her husband.

Herr Schmidt left in the back of a truck the next day, heading for another camp where they wouldn't know he was married and had a family. A letter came from him, three weeks later. Frau Schmidt opened it, read it, and then looked up at Johannes and Helga.

'Not America,' she said. 'It would take six months before he could go to America, so many want to go there. But the men at that camp say he can go to a place called Australia now.'

Australia! Johannes remembered the sailor's lessons. 'That is on the other side of the world! Not just one ocean to cross, but lots!'

Frau Schmidt bit her lip. 'If he thinks Australia is best, then it must be. And if it's not good, then one day we can maybe go to America instead.'

You could stay here, thought Johannes. Your home may be under Russian control now, but there are other places in Germany. So much must be rebuilt now that surely you would find a home in a few months, a year at most, and Herr Schmidt would find a job.

But he said nothing. For Frau Schmidt, Germany would always be the land of war, of loss. And Herr Schmidt knew it.

And Helga?

Johannes realised he had never heard Helga mourn the loss of anything, or any place or any person, except for Hannes. It was as if Helga had wiped the professor's box of sand smooth, with no memories left on it at all.

Chapter 27

JOHANNES
GERMANY, 1948

Yet another year in the camp for those labelled DP. More refugees had come. More had left. Notes of hope and names and longing still hung on doorposts, even trees. Every day someone in the camp learned of a relative alive, and cried for joy, or one who had died, or one who had been alive a year ago and might …

So many, many 'mights'.

The food was a little more plentiful, with potatoes and corned beef and carrots in the midday stew, and bread that was bread, instead of bran and sawdust, and sometimes even a scrape of butter or margarine.

But little else changed. There were too few places, it seemed, for the displaced to go.

Helga and Johannes still attended the makeshift school, with teachers stripped of all but their learning and their wish to share — to give, perhaps, a chance of life to those who were young, and still might have a life to live beyond the DP camp.

Sometimes a few other young people joined them, but not often. Most young people lived for the day, scavenging beyond the camp for goods to trade, or to brighten small grey lives. Others lived in no time, but simply sat and stared: children unable to bear the past, who had no future to imagine, who found even the present terrifying, waking each day not knowing what new faces might arrive, what familiar ones might vanish. Whether, among the new faces, old tormentors might appear, for even Nazis and concentration camp guards could now be called displaced. What could you do, if a demon from your past appeared?

Nothing. Eat your bread and margarine. Drink your stew, your ersatz coffee, sleep in your bunk; accept the nightmares of day as well as darkness. And so children sat unmoving, not looking up or even glancing at the tears upon their mothers' faces, as they tried to spoon in food or water, to wake their children into the land of now.

Frau Schmidt still sewed. She had earned a small store of jewellery, which kept its value better than German paper money. Helga helped her and so did Johannes, in the days they did not help at the hospital. It was embarrassing for a boy to hold a needle, so he helped make patterns from old newspaper and cut cloth and unpicked seams from rags that might become new dresses or shirts, or unravelled and rolled the yarn of jumpers. Old blankets could become coats, embroidered till they looked bright and even fashionable, the designs discovered in newspapers or magazines months old by the time they saw them. Old handbags, boots or lederhosen could be cut into small patches of leather, sewn together and remade as new.

But where Helga worked, so did Johannes. Where Johannes worked, Helga came too. Partly it was to talk English together, for Helga would need English if — when — she and Frau Schmidt could join Herr Schmidt in Australia. But mostly it was because they had faced death together and chosen life, and worked out how to keep it; and every day that they survived in this camp was another that they survived together.

We fit together, me and Helga, thought Johannes. Not just what we have been through, but the way we want to learn things, the way we both find work satisfying. A whisper inside him said, 'Working helps keep nightmares away.'

Perhaps it did for Helga too.

A letter arrived from Herr Schmidt in Italy, and then one from Malta, and then one posted in a town called Fremantle in Australia and, finally, from a place called Eucumbene, way on the other side of the big island continent.

Dear Marta and Helga,

I hope you are both well, as I am well. You will be as surprised as I am to see the address on this letter. I am working as a labourer on a project to build a tunnel through a mountain to channel water from a river called the Snowy River to make hydro-electricity and then irrigate the dry land to grow vegetables. There is much dry land in Australia.

It seems that despite what the men from Australia told me, Australia does not recognise my engineering papers. I will have to do more exams, but to do them my English must be better. Till then, I work here, and I practise my English. But the Australian engineers here are friendly and have lent me their textbooks, so I hope that before the year is out I will be an engineer again.

Meanwhile we live in huts, and it is cold. But the food is plentiful, though always sheep or rabbit, but we have meat and butter at every meal, and white bread, and any man may have as much food as he wishes to eat. There are men here from every country on earth.

This is not a place for families, although Sister Bernadette is setting up a school for the camp children. But when I am an engineer and have engineer's wages, not a labourer's pay, we can rent a house in Cooma, which is a bigger town, with better schools, and when my three years are up working in the country we can live in Sydney. I saw it only briefly but it is a beautiful city, and I am sure we can be happy there. Surely by then families will be allowed to join their men in Australia. The government cannot be so cruel as to keep us all apart!

I remain,
your loving husband and father,
Ernst Schmidt

'I wonder if he has seen a kangaroo,' said Helga. The sailor had told them about kangaroos, and savage koalas that dropped on your head and tried to smother you, and things called boomerangs that Australians threw to hit each other on the head, but then the boomerang came back to the hand of the person who had thrown it.

Australia sounded odd. But there had been no bombing in southern Australia, no occupying troops, no bands of soldiers looting. Boomerangs sounded better than rifles and machine guns.

Australians played cricket too, the sailor had said, and all went to the beach in swimming costumes and played in the waves. Herr Schmidt had not mentioned any of those.

'Do you think he is happy there?' whispered Frau Schmidt.

'I think he misses his family,' said Helga softly. 'But he can see a future now. A good one. A home in a city he says is beautiful.'

Frau Schmidt smiled at her. 'And good schools for you.'

Helga met Johannes's eyes. 'I think our school here is the best one in the world.'

Vati and Mutti sat with Johannes in the dining room that evening after dinner, when most of the others had left.

'Herr Schmidt has his engineer's certificate,' said Vati. He took Mutti's hand. 'And even then they will not let him work at his profession. All we have are pieces of paper that call us DPs. Nothing to prove our qualifications at all.'

'But you work as doctors now!' cried Johannes.

Vati shrugged. 'We are allowed to work here because other doctors do not want to work in a DP camp, for Pfennigs and turnip stew. If the Australians will not let Herr Schmidt be an engineer, even on a project that so badly needs engineers, they will not let us practise medicine.'

'And why would we want to go to Australia?' asked Mutti. 'It is a land of convicts, English prisoners sent out to a land no one else wanted, a land of desert and savages.'

'Herr Schmidt says Sydney is beautiful,' began Johannes.

'Herr Schmidt wishes to give his family hope,' said Mutti gently. 'He is in Australia now, and must make the best of it.'

'How many million DPs must Australia sort through until they say welcome to families?' said Vati. 'Will it take ten years? Never, perhaps. But if I go to England as a single man, I can work for two years, and get my residency, and then I can send for you. Or I might go to America or Canada or Brazil.'

'They would all be better places to live than Australia,' said Mutti.

'Can we really never go home?' asked Johannes in a small voice.

Vati took his hand. 'There are bad stories from new refugees who have escaped from the Russian territories. There are gangs of ruffians and even less food than here. Whoever has the land where our hospital and home were may think we have come back to claim it and denounce us as criminals or traitors, to be sent to a Russian prison camp. It wasn't safe three years ago; it is even less safe now.' He met Mutti's eyes. 'We survived a German extermination camp. Would we survive a Russian one?'

'But what if America or Canada or Brazil will not let you be doctors?' demanded Johannes.

'They are older nations than Australia, more civilised. There would be more choice of jobs there. Perhaps I might be a salesman for medical supplies.' Vati lifted his chin. 'We have survived, Johannes. Whatever is before us now, we will survive that too.'

'And one day,' said Mutti quietly, 'we will have a new home.'

'A house,' said Vati, 'a house of our own. A cat ...'

For a moment Johannes thought he meant a cat to eat, if they were hungry. But then he remembered Maus. A cat who you fed, because there was so much food a cat could eat some too.

'England would be good,' he ventured, remembering the English major who had been kind. 'Or America,' remembering the American who gave him chewing gum. There would be more to eat in America, perhaps ...

But Vati did not go to America. For a letter came from Frau Marks.

Chapter 28

FRAU MARKS
ENGLAND, SEPTEMBER 1947

Mrs Marks sat in the library café and read the letter again. She sat there every morning now, eating toast and tea. It was all she did: eat slowly, through the day. Miriam said she needed building up. She must be strong for Georg.

But Georg was gone. Gone forever. Had she been so silly that she had dreamed she would hold him in her arms, her little boy?

Little boys grow up. The little boy had vanished. Not just from childhood, but from England, to Australia at the other end of the world, where Miriam had sent him to be safe.

She wanted to be angry with Miriam. She could not. Miriam had done what must be done. If Georg had stayed in England, he might have died in an air raid; might have been imprisoned as an enemy if the British had found out he was Georg, not George.

Georg was safe in Australia. No, George was safe. Georg was gone.

'Another cup of tea, love?'

'Yes, please.' Mrs Huntley was so kind. The tea would be mostly hot water, vaguely burned-toast colour, but it helped her to swallow the bread. Soon she would have false teeth, Miriam had promised, and would be able to eat more than toast soaked in tea, and soup, which was all she could manage since her teeth had fallen out from starvation in the camps.

'Is that a letter from your boy, love? George? George used to come into my library every day, till it was bombed and we moved the books in here. I write to him at Christmas still, and send him a book too. He loves his books.'

She tried not to be jealous of this woman who had known her son when he was ten, eleven. Months, years, gone from her life. Time she could never have.

'Yes. It's from Georg ... George.'

'Well, I would never have guessed he was German. But it explains things too. He was such a quiet one. Give him my love.'

No hatred because Georg was German. None for her either. But they had been rejected by Germany, both of them — perhaps that meant something to this woman here. Or maybe, like Sister Columba, she gave love instead of hate.

Mrs Marks looked down at the letter once again, the letter she had read a thousand times since he had sent it to her two years ago, would read a thousand more, would read to this kind woman here just for the joy and pain of hearing her son's words aloud.

Dear Mutti,

I am so glad you are alive. I knew you were, but it is good to know for sure. Mud always said you were alive too. She cried when Aunt Miriam sent the telegram, and so did Auntie Thel. I cried too. You will like Auntie Thel and Uncle Ron and Mud, and her family too.

Uncle Ron says that Aunt Miriam may have told you this already. It will be easier for you to get a ship to Australia than for me to come to England. Ships go from Australia to England full of machinery and wheat and wool, and so there is much more room on them on the way back here than when they go to you. Aunt Miriam thinks you might be able to get a passage to Australia by the end of the year, but it might be two years before I could come to you in England.

But that is not why I hope that you will come here. I am not German now, and I was never English. I am Australian. My family is here too. They will be your family as well. In England we have only Aunt Miriam and her little flat, but here we have a big house with plenty of room for you too. In a few years I will probably get a scholarship to go to university, which will pay enough for me to stay in Sydney at a college. Mud is certain to get a scholarship too. We are ridiculously intelligent, Mud says. You will like Mud very much. Her real name is Maud, but that is a long funny story I will tell you another time. You will really like Mud.

Please, come here. If you ask me to, I will come to England. But I am happy here, and you will be too.

Here is a photo of us all last Christmas. I love you. Mud sends her love too, and Auntie Thel and Uncle Ron and Mud's mum and dad and brothers.

Love,
George

She looked at the photo again. She wished yet again for colours but, even without them, you could see the sky was blue and cloudless, not endless grey. The verandah was deep, the woman elderly but wearing a good dress with pearls; the man grey-haired, in a shirt and tie but no coat. But they were primitive in Australia, she knew that ...

She had not been able to get a passage on a ship to Australia yet. The places were reserved for soldiers and war brides, not mothers. And Georg should come to Oxford. He would get a proper education there. What university did Sydney have?

A good one, Miriam had said. Miriam knew these things. Miriam wept for her lost brother; wept each night when she thought her sister-in-law was asleep. But she had said too that Georg should not come here.

Australia was his life now.

Her son had a life.

If she were to have a life again, it must be there.

Chapter 29

She shared a cabin with three other women, a two-berth cabin forced to fit four. She spoke little, but listened to their chatter: war brides, married to Australian airmen or soldiers who had been stationed in England, fallen in love and married there. They were going to love, marriage, children, happiness, decades holding hands each night or holding conversations over breakfast.

Their lives were in front of them. Hers had emptied, bit by bit. All that was left now was Georg.

George. She had to call him George. His whole childhood had been taken from her, even the name she and Simon had chosen for him. Stolen from her, given to these people in Australia, who she could not hate for they were good people who had given her son joy.

How could she talk to these young women, chatting of lipsticks carefully saved for the moment they met their husbands again, setting each other's hair, resewing their old dresses to make their trousseaux?

Her clothes were Miriam's, made to fit her by a little refugee dressmaker in a room that sweated damp; a refugee like her, head down at her sewing machine as if she were sewing a new life, not just taking in clothes to fit a too-thin woman.

'Don't take them in too much,' Miriam had said. 'And leave decent seams — you can let them out when you put on weight.'

Would she put on weight? Probably, even on this ship with its potatoes and corned meat for every meal. But could she 'put on' life?

She didn't know.

A thin, blue-green line of coast appeared between the sea and sky. The other passengers shrieked with excitement. She stayed numb.

They docked at Fremantle. The sky was the wrong colour, the light too bright, though that might be the reflection from the sea. She didn't go ashore. Georg — *George* — was still a continent away. She had no curiosity to see country she'd never see again.

Along southern Australia; now there were white and rust-coloured cliffs, a pod of whales. Not long now. She thought: I should be excited. She was not. She felt like a surgery patient where too much had been removed to feel that what was left was real.

Melbourne, where again she could have gone ashore for half a day but didn't. She stayed on board, glad of the cabin to herself. Then more blue-green coast, a too-small gap in great brown cliffs but the ship managed to fit through, the shock of a calm harbour, peninsulas of trees running down into the sea, and surprisingly tidy streets of houses and ferries bobbing on the waves.

Had she expected convict huts? Farms? She realised she had not even tried to find out about Sydney. Reality was not this world of light and fishermen wearing shorts in dinghies waving at the ship, excited women on the deck waving back. Reality was camps in battered Europe, her friends still hungry, starving …

She blinked, to try to see the shining harbour, but all she saw was them. She had wired money to yet another contact of Miriam's, to give to the Wolchekis and Schmidts, to buy them extra food, if it could be had. For she had money now, not just the jewellery and papers she had hidden at the hospital. The driver had taken her to her house, their house, hers and Simon's and Georg's. It was still there, even the flowers in the garden; and, when she knocked, Gudrun answered the door.

They stared at each other, sister to sister, one in a good suit — faded but still good — with pearls, the other in clothes carefully resewn from grey rags and fallen-out hair that had not yet grown back, fingers like a skeleton's with half the nails worn away.

Frau Marks said, 'This is my house.' Because this was the woman who refused to shelter her and her son, who had spat at her for marrying a Jude.

'Our house was bombed,' said Gudrun.

They did not hug or kiss or cry. Nor did they reproach each other. It was as if a vast wall of emotion had built up between them, so big that if either showed anger or fear the whole great structure would tumble and flatten them both.

'I have the title deeds to this house,' said Frau Marks.

'We have nowhere else to go.' It was not quite a plea.

Frau Marks nodded. 'But you agree, this is my house?'

'Yes.'

'Then you will pay rent —' and, as Gudrun opened her mouth to speak, 'when you are able.'

And then she left, walking in her grey dress that had been rags, trying not to shuffle in her too-big shoes, back to the English driver and the English car.

She had discovered that in England too Simon had property and money from his parents' estate. She had known Simon's family was well off, but like most women had left all money matters to her husband.

She did not know if the inheritance was enough to keep her secure for all her life. Money had new meaning in this post-war world. Nor could she turn the property into money, not in the chaos of post-war England. But there would be enough, she thought, to buy a small house in Australia, for Georg to study whatever he wished, and money to send to the Wolchekis and the Schmidts.

The ship veered. She could see the docks now, the crush of people.

And suddenly she was *here*, not there. Excitement beat like a drum, her heart too big for her still-thin body. Was Georg on the wharf?

She tried to push her way up to the railing, but she was still too weak. At last she gave up, went back to her cabin and fetched her suitcase — she had no trunk — and took her place in the line. Another line after so many lines. But would there be life at the end of this one?

She didn't know. She didn't know. If she shut her eyes, she could still hear chanting, 'Jude, Jude ...' still see Simon fall, see the children huddled in the cellar, see Sister Columba lying on the wooden bunk, her blistered arms around Johannes.

She had not even lit a candle for Sister Columba, nor even prayed for her. It was as if her soul was dead. The only warmth was hatred.

The line inched forwards. At last she reached the gangplank. Her case was heavy in her hand. She walked, head down. Do not attract attention; do not look up. Do not meet their eyes. It took nine months to bear a child. A lifetime to love them. The two years in England had not been long enough to undo six years of terror and loss. Nor were they long enough to reclaim a life.

'Mutti!'

Frau Marks lifted her eyes.

Her son smiled back.

Her son was a blue-eyed toddler, waddling towards her; he was the proud boy in his cap, off to school; the stoic, frightened child she had last farewelled.

Here stood a handsome young man, his hand held tightly by a young woman with tanned skin and badly cut hair and green eyes that challenged the world.

Her son. All of them her son. The girl's other hand held one half of a banner, *Welcome, Mutti!* and, in smaller letters, *Welcome, Mrs Marks!* The other end was held by an elderly man in a good suit, next to an elderly woman well dressed in gloves and hat and handbag and wearing pearls. And all of them smiling, smiling, so happy and rejoicing, so … so clean …

And she was dirty. Not with the filth of one camp, finally washed off, and the grime of another, where washing was restricted to once a week, but with a soul that was black with hatred, raw with pain. She could not step forwards, hug this handsome boy, the boy who looked at her with love.

She shut her eyes, saw herself grab shears, the kind for pruning hedges. She hacked at the hatred in her soul, fast and frantic, let it fly back across the ocean to the land where it belonged.

She opened her eyes, put down her suitcase, opened her arms, her heart.

She held her son, her loving son. She held her son with love.

Chapter 30

JOHANNES
GERMANY, MAY 1948

'*Dear Doktors Wolcheki and Johannes, I hope that you are well, and that my parcels and letters to you have arrived. I have been concerned not to hear from you, but did receive a letter from Herr Schmidt, who assured me he had heard from his wife and daughter that you are well and still at the camp …*'

Mutti glanced at Vati. Vati shrugged. Parcels sometimes arrived, but none had come especially for them. With Germany starving, bombed and desperate, most packages were stolen long before they reached those they had been sent to, especially DPs.

But this letter had not come with a parcel, so it had got through.

I have settled more happily in Australia than when I first wrote to you. The accent is strange — Australians swallow half their words — and their only cooking is boiling vegetables and grilling or roasting sheep, sheep and still more sheep, chops and legs and shoulders, and the sausages are mostly bread, not meat, even in this land of meat, and taste of nothing. Yet they are kind. Indeed, I have met nothing but kindness since I have been here.

I have been living with Georg's foster parents as I explained in my last letter, though I must call him George now, as that is the name he has chosen. But soon he and his friend Maud will go to the University of Sydney. George wishes to study law and Maud to study psychology. I have decided, therefore, to buy a small house, near the university, where they can stay with me.

My late husband's father left property for us in England, and I was also able to find the valuables I had hidden when I fled my home in Germany, after my husband was killed. My sister-in-law, Miriam, is also most generous, as she says we are the only family she has and she thinks of George as a son. My son, it seems, is very rich in family, and that family have extended their arms to me too.

Now George's Australian family wish to extend those arms to you. When I told the Peaslakes about you, Mr Peaslake told me firmly that they wish to sponsor you — all three of you — to come to Australia. If you have a sponsor, then you may get a permit to come as a family.

I wrote to Miriam, explaining your situation. She works in the government and has influence and connections. I told her you had met while doing post-graduate medical studies at the University of Edinburgh. She was able to get copies of your graduation documents and, due to the kind work of Mr Peaslake, I attach a letter from the Medical Board of Australia that states that, given your UK postgraduate qualifications, you will be permitted to practise medicine in Australia, provided you can pass an exam in English. I am sure that as you passed the university exams in Edinburgh, your English will be more than adequate for Australia!

You should be contacted by the Australian Embassy shortly — indeed, you may have already been contacted, as I know how unreliable the mail can be.

Australia may be strange — even the trees are the wrong colour, more grey-blue than green. But much of it is beautiful, and it is safe and far away from horrors. I think you will be happy here, as I am now. Mr Peaslake wishes me to say that he and his wife would be happy for you to stay with them, if you wish to practise in a small country town. But if you wish to live and work in Sydney, I would be most happy for you to stay with me for as long as you wish. Housing is in short supply here and it is easier to buy a house than rent one. But be assured that there will be a home and jobs and a welcome, whatever you decide.

From your affectionate friend,
Frau Marks (Nurse Stöhlich)

Chapter 31

'Goodbye,' he said to Helga.

It wasn't enough. He wanted to hug her, hold her, stay with her forever. Because even if they were sailing to freedom now, this was still the belly of the ogre where anything could happen, and only Helga was the rock that never changed, kind Helga with the gentle hands, Helga with a mind that hunted like his own, Helga, the always friend.

'Goodbye,' said Helga tightly, as if she too refused to cry.

But she would come to Australia too, one day. Australia was a big place, but they would find each other. They had found their families before in the chaos of war and its aftermath. They would find each other again.

Frau Schmidt pressed a parcel into his hands, wrapped in many-times-used brown paper. 'A new shirt for you, and one for your father. A pretty dress for your mother. All from new fabric too! You must look good on the ship.'

The tears that prickled behind his eyelids began to flow, but to wipe them would just show everyone that he was crying. How many hours had Frau Schmidt and Helga worked in secret to make these for them? How many loaves of bread, sausages and hunks of cheese would they not eat, to give them clothes made of new material?

'We will see you in Australia,' said Mutti, in her new coat made from an old blanket, embroidered at the collar and cuffs. She too seemed near to tears. 'Surely they will let families come soon. And if they don't, we will persuade the Peaslakes to send permits for you.'

'By Christmas!' said Johannes desperately, his cheeks cold with tears. 'We will see you by Christmas!'

He and Mutti and Vati clambered into the truck, sitting with its exhaust steaming among the snowdrifts. No suitcases, but brown-paper parcels at least, instead of the ragged bundles they had come with. Hunger instead of the starvation they had felt back then. Apprehension instead of terror. This was better. It must be better!

Why then was he so afraid?

The truck stopped at the railway station. Hands helped them down. Johannes followed Mutti and Vati along the path through the snow to the railway platform.

He stopped. Terror fell like a black blanket. He could not go on. He shut his eyes.

'Johannes,' whispered Mutti.

No! Cattle cars and bodies. The stench of corpses rotting, of days-old faeces, of women and children crushed together, the dreams from his delirium ...

'Johannes,' said Mutti again softly, and he could hear the fear in her voice too.

Suddenly it was as if Helga held his hand, as she had held it through so many horrors. He opened his eyes. No cattle cars. Just ordinary railway carriages, with proper seats, and even a buffet car serving coffee. Vati showed the tickets the Australians had sent to them to the conductor, who opened the carriage door.

They sat, on bench seats of real leather, their embarrassing brown-paper parcels up on the luggage rack among the proper luggage.

The train moved.

Past the platform, past snowy meadows and evergreen forest dappled white. A deer looked at the train curiously, then bent to eat.

Villages, old, unscarred. Villages, with makeshift houses rising from the rubble. A conductor in a uniform came along the passage. He opened the door to their compartment.

Johannes froze. The conductor was going to order them out. To a cattle car, further down the train. Make them get off at the next station, go to another camp, a labour camp … It had all been another trick to get them to leave the DP camp with no fuss or argument.

'Dinner in half an hour in the dining car,' said the conductor.

White linen tablecloths. A proper soup spoon. Thin clear soup, not even any turnip in it. They would starve, on soup like this, all the way to the ship to Australia waiting at Naples!

Mutti picked up a roll of white bread from her side plate. Johannes hadn't noticed they each had one. She broke off a piece and spread on butter. Real butter.

The waiter took the soup plates. He brought back other plates, filled with food.

Johannes had forgotten that meals could have more than one dish. He had to remind himself how to use a knife and fork, instead of just a spoon.

'Goulash,' said Mutti wonderingly, taking a mouthful. There was so much meat, covered in sour-cream sauce coloured deep red by paprika and served with noodles. He felt slightly sick from such rich food, but could not stop eating.

The waiter took their empty plates, then came back again. 'Cherry strudel ...' whispered Johannes. Just as they'd had at home.

He glanced at Mutti, saw her tears. She buried her head in Vati's shoulder. Vati held her, hugged her, took Johannes's hand across the table. Cherry strudel ...

Mutti glanced at the other women in the buffet car. 'I wish I had gloves,' she whispered. 'A proper hat.'

Vati smiled, but his smile held pain. 'No one wears gloves in the dining car.'

Mutti nodded. But she kept her hands in her pockets when other women were nearby.

Their bunks on the train were narrow, rattling, shaking as the train snorted through the night. Bunks with sheets and quilts and pillows, coffee and rolls and jam for breakfast, the crumpled nations of Europe rattling by, interspersed with forest, deer sometimes, or hare, and once a Wildschwein, a sow, followed by her piglets, uninterested in the train and its passengers.

The trees in Australia are grey-blue, he thought, with strange animals called kangaroos and murderous koalas. Were there even cats, in Australia? The sailor hadn't seen a cat on his brief stay in Australia; nor were there any books in the camp that might have told him more.

Goodbye, green trees, he thought. Goodbye, deer and Wildschweine. Goodbye, Helga.

No! For he would see her soon. He must! All the rest ... he was glad to see it go. Its beauty had tricked him for a moment, to think it was a land of safety, kindness and rules. The belly of the ogre had no rules.

Soon, soon, they'd leave the ogre far behind.

Chapter 32

JOHANNES
EUROPE, 1949

Night. The train rattled, engine snorting. Men yelled outside.

Johannes struggled from his bunk just as a man with a strange English accent walked along the aisle. 'No worries,' he called out. 'Everyone stay calm. The Russian soldiers just want to see your papers.' A Russian guard followed the Australian — he must be Australian, thought Johannes, though he wore no uniform. The guard called the same instruction in German.

And then more Russians came along. Big men, in shabby uniforms, with angry eyes. They snatched the papers, examined them, thrust them back, person after person.

'What are they looking for?' whispered Johannes as the soldiers headed to the next carriage.

'People who are trying to escape from Russian-occupied territory,' Mutti whispered back.

'People like us?'

She crossed to his bunk and put her arms around him. 'No. We have DP papers and Australian papers. The Russians cannot know that we came from Poland.'

Johannes nodded. But he could feel her fear. Smell the fear of all of the passengers, only easing as the train plunged into darkness again.

Another warning at breakfast. 'The Italian Red Army Brigade has units in this area. Everyone stay low on the floor. If you must move, stay away from the windows.'

They cowered on the floor for an hour. Two hours. Johannes wanted the toilet — he should not have had the second cup of cocoa at breakfast. Suddenly the train halted. Rifles were thrust through the windows, and then men's faces. Johannes heard a woman scream in another carriage.

The men shouted, gesturing at the passengers, but they spoke in Italian, which no one understood.

Or if they did, like Vati, they did not translate.

Five minutes. Six. The train clanked and began to move. The men withdrew their rifles, jeering as the train left.

The country changed again. Villages that were mostly rubble, with no attempt yet to rebuild them. Farmhouses no bigger than a cow byre. Every hill was planted with olives or grapevines. Each time they stopped at a station, men and women with careworn faces smiled and handed them oranges as presents with cries of 'Buona fortuna!' and 'Australia!' Italians joined the train now, heading to the ship to Australia.

Johannes could hardly remember what an orange tasted like. It was sweet sunlight, he decided, and ate another and another, and two more after that. The other passengers in the carriage smiled at the boy so dedicatedly eating oranges, and gave him most of theirs too.

The final DP camp was near Naples, tucked below the mighty volcano that had buried the Roman city of Pompeii. Even that early in the year it was so warm they took off their overcoats.

The camp was ... a camp. Bunk beds. This one had a kitchen too, where people could make their own cocoa or even other meals, as well as a dining room.

They sat there the first morning with ersatz coffee and bread and margarine, the same as at the other camp. Even the official who marched into the hall looked the same, though he spoke in English. 'The ship is not ready. I'm sorry. You will need to stay here till it is.'

Vati stood up. 'How long?'

The man shrugged. 'Three weeks? Six weeks? Materials are short just now — you must know that.'

All around, people translated for each other. Vati sat down.

No one grumbled. No one shouted, 'You have tricked us! Give us our ship!'

The people in that dining room were experts in waiting. Nor had they a choice.

So they waited. The food was poor: pasta like lumps of glue, sauces with no meat, just bread and margarine and watery stews of vegetables again. But they were free to roam outside the camp, up the steep slopes of the volcano, strange red pebbles on either side, the giant caldera steaming gently, splattered with yellow crystals; hills of olive groves and vast stretches of tomatoes. Some of the camp inmates visited Pompeii.

'It will be educational,' said Mutti half-heartedly.

They did not go. They had no wish to see more ruins, even ancient ones.

And then, at last, the ship.

Chapter 33

JOHANNES
VOYAGE TO AUSTRALIA, 1949

The ship smelled of salt and fresh paint and sawdust. It took a whole day to assign everyone to their quarters. Johannes's family were given a tiny cabin to themselves, on the lowest level. Single men slept in the hold and single women shared cabins.

Johannes gazed at his bunk. It was a good bunk, with new-looking sheets and blankets. One day, he thought, I will have a proper bed.

He joined the crowds up on deck as the Italians on the docks cheered and waved goodbye. Engines vibrated, then silently the ship drew out of the harbour and, as night fell about them, glided south under an umbrella of stars.

The bell rang for dinner. Tables! Proper tables, not benches. Starched linen tablecloths, proper knives and forks, Italian waiters bringing proper food — real bread and butter — butter, not margarine! And if the meat was mostly corned beef, it was meat, and the potatoes were roasted till they were crisp.

People laughed. It unnerved him. Every few nights the DPs held a concert. An Australian delegation on board joined in, performing cabaret songs or dancing or reciting poems in English, which volunteers in the audience had to translate.

Every day, up on deck, the Australian delegation members were surrounded by people asking questions.

'Why does Australia want so many DPs when America and England take so few?'

'Is Australia beautiful?'

'Can I be an architect there, as I was before the war?'

'Don't worry about it,' said the Australians. 'Of course you can practise your professions in Australia. Australia is the best country in the world. The weather is as warm as Naples and there are beaches everywhere, with sunshine and golden sand. Australians believe in a fair go for everyone. No worries! In five years you will become Australians too!'

Johannes listened. He didn't quite believe it all. An Australian delegation had told Herr Schmidt he could be an engineer once he was there. They had either lied or been wrong.

Were they lying now? Perhaps all officials lied, in Australia too. Perhaps there were no beaches, just sheer cliffs and rock, and desert like it said on the map.

The Australians had not mentioned desert.

The ship sailed on, stopping at ports before the final vast ocean to Australia. But they had little money to spend ashore. And what if the ship sailed without them? Life was too precarious to risk a trip ashore.

The ship creaked and groaned through a rising sea. A passenger, a man, was washed overboard, and a sailor too, lost in a storm. Johannes, Mutti and Vati stayed in their cabin. Vati ventured out once a day to bring back water — when you were seasick, it was important to keep up your fluids — and bread, because bread helped line the stomach.

The air grew thick. Johannes gasped for breath. At first he thought that he was sick, that Mutti was sick and Vati too. They all had sweat upon their foreheads.

The door opened and a steward looked in. 'Better get on deck, mateys. The engines are crook and the air-conditioning has broken down.'

Up onto the rain-wet, sea-wet decks. Drinking water was scarce now too. The family huddled under a bench on deck most of the day, as well as night, visiting their cabin only to change into less damp clothes. I thought we were leaving the ogre behind, thought Johannes numbly. Perhaps when an ogre swallows you there never is a true escape.

He was too old to think about ogres now, he told himself. But the ogre had gripped him too long.

The ship sailed on, their cabin still too stuffy to sleep in. More sea and sky. They had been sailing for six weeks now.

Someone cheered on one of the higher decks. A face appeared, upside down, peering at the family huddled under the bench. 'Come on. Land!'

Johannes struggled to his feet, while Vati helped Mutti up.

'Land!' A wall of people stood along the deck, peering at grey sea, at clouded sky. And darker grey shadow that might be land or storm cloud split the horizon.

The shadow grew as the ship sailed on. By afternoon the sky had turned blue. The land became a headland: treeless, barren, the colour of dirt that'd had all its goodness washed away. Johannes stared at it in horror.

But the ship sailed past the barren headland. At last he could see trees, greener than he had expected. A port called Fremantle —

which was in Australia, but further from where they were going than the German camp had been from Naples.

The ship's engines vibrated to life again. They sailed once more. Fog fell, shrouding them as the ship coasted onwards, onwards. They might have been heading anywhere. Once again they were just parcels, bundles of meat, helpless. DPs to be taken where their captors willed.

They slept under the bench again, huddled together. When Johannes woke, they were in Melbourne.

Chapter 34

The wharf teemed with ants — tall lean ants with tanned skin and short haircuts, bustling here and there and pushing trolleys, lifting sacks. The skin around their eyes was wrinkled, as if they had had to squeeze their eyes to slits against the sun for so long. But most of the faces seemed kind.

The passengers lined up. They waited. They marched. All of them were well practised in lining up, in waiting, in marching, in showing papers as they were herded onto a bus, and then to a railway station.

It was not a cattle car. Nor was there a dining car, just bench seats. But they were comfortable and the wood was polished, and Johannes could open the window when the smoke from the engine wasn't blowing their way, and gaze out.

Flat land. Brown grass. Square fields with nothing but cows or sheep inside. A few farmhouses, with corrugated-iron roofs, more like barracks than proper homes. Spiky grass and skinnier trees, the wrong colour, as Nurse Stöhlich ... Frau Marks ... had said.

The train stopped. Passengers got off to use the toilet, to line up on the station platform in front of tables made cheerful with bright tablecloths, with smiling women in floral dresses serving the passengers. 'Here you are, love,' said one, handing Johannes a parcel of sandwiches wrapped in paper, an apple and a big wedge of cake.

She called me 'love', thought Johannes as he walked back to the train. An Australian called me 'love'.

Perhaps Frau Marks was right and one could live in this strange ugly land.

The next stop, at Albury, was the last stop on the train. They lined up, they waited, they marched. They showed their papers and boarded a bus.

Another camp, called Bonegilla — a weird name that meant nothing to the newcomers. A camp that was just a camp, with round-roofed metal barracks and bunks, except this camp had no fences. Cows grazed around the buildings. At night they licked the moisture off the outside walls, *scritch*, *slurp*, *scratch*.

The camp was cold — as cold as the DP camp, so again they had to wear all their clothes all day and night — but here there was no snow to make the world look bright, though for the first hour or so after sunrise the world glittered with frost. At night Johannes's spit froze to the pillow. He had to remove the tiny icicle from the fabric each morning, so it could melt.

A dining room. No tablecloths but good food. Frau Marks had been right there too. Sheep meat, three times a day, chops with eggs and chips for breakfast. Chops with eggs and chips for lunch. Chops with eggs and chips for dinner, and all the leftovers were thrown away, not even fed to pigs or hens.

Johannes thought of Helga, hungry back in the camp in the green forest, where it would be summer now. The leftovers from his family's meal alone, the fatty tails from the chops, the too-browned chips, would have fed her family for the whole day.

At least, though, now he could write to her. The Australians gave each inmate five shillings a week, enough to take the bus to Albury, to buy a milkshake and chocolate and stamps, a pen and ink and paper and an envelope.

Dear Helga,
   I hope that you are well.
   We are in Australia.

Johannes tried to think what he should say now. He could not say how strange Australia was, because unless Herr Schmidt had decided to leave when his three years' service was up, Helga and Frau Schmidt must come here too. He didn't want them to be afraid. Nor could he lie to Helga. And maybe things would be better in Sydney, as Frau Marks said.

There is meat three times a day, and always sheep, as Frau Marks told us, but there are cows here too, so sometimes there must be beef. There is a lot of milk. I drink it five times a day, as Mutti says it will help my bones grow. I didn't think I would ever get bored eating meat and drinking milk, but now I am.

The Australians are friendly. I saw six kangaroos on the train journey from Melbourne. They are bigger than I thought, some taller than Vati, but the train conductor said they mostly do not attack people but run away. I asked him about the savage koalas and he laughed, and said it was a joke, and not to worry, that koalas are just soft and fluffy and sit and eat gum leaves and sleep all day. He said people have cats in Australia too. I think I would like a cat again, and there is a lot of meat here to feed a pet.

I visited the library in Albury. It was strange to be surrounded by walls of books again. It was so good I just sat there, and only remembered to find a book to read half an hour before I had to leave to catch the bus.

Soon we will go to Sydney. I will write from there.

He wanted to write, *Love from Johannes*, but that might seem too … forward. He wrote instead, *Yours, always, Johannes*. Then he sealed the envelope and posted it in the red letter box before they took the bus back to the camp.

~❦~

The next day Vati argued with the Australian officials. So did Mutti. Every inmate had to put down their profession, to be assigned to jobs.

Doctor, wrote Vati.

The official stared. 'You can't put *doctor*! All the men must write *labourer* and the women must put *domestic servant*.'

'I am not a labourer,' said Vati angrily. 'I am a doctor, and I have English papers that say I am.'

Mutti took the pen and wrote *doctor* too.

'But a sheila can't be a doctor!' expostulated the official.

'But I am,' said Mutti, and her voice was steel. 'I have been a doctor in Edinburgh, a doctor in Poland, a doctor in a camp run by the Nazis, a doctor in a camp run by the Americans, and a doctor in another run by the United Nations and the English. I would not let the Nazis stop me being a doctor. I will not let you.'

'But we don't have jobs for —' began the official.

'We have jobs waiting for us. And a place to live,' said Vati calmly.

'What the heck ... have it your own way!' The man waved them through.

A bus again. Another railway platform, not the one they had arrived on, because in this strange land it seemed the railway tracks were different in Melbourne and in Sydney, and you must change onto different trains to get from one to the other.

More brown paddocks and more cows and sheep. Brown streams and forests of white-trunked trees and tin-roofed houses sitting in more brown paddocks. Night fell before they reached the outskirts of Sydney. All Johannes could see from the train were streets with streetlights, and lighted kitchens with people eating dinner in them.

But they were eating, with tables and stoves and curtains at the windows. He hadn't seen bomb damage, nor were there soldiers stopping trains to check their papers, nor savages or bands of convicts holding them up to steal all they had, their brown-paper packages even more stained from the voyage. Even the officious man at the Bonegilla camp had not punished Vati or Mutti for insisting they were doctors.

The train drew up in a cloud of steam. And there, on the platform, in a pretty coat not made from a blanket, and her hair short and curled, was Frau Marks, wearing lipstick and totally different and totally the same, smiling, waving and, beside her, a tall boy and a skinny girl with tanned skin, smiling and waving too, and an elderly couple with smiles as bright as the moon.

For the first time Johannes thought: Perhaps this might be good.

Chapter 35

JOHANNES
AUSTRALIA, 1949–1950

Frau Marks's house was shabby, but big enough for them all. She and Mud shared a bedroom, and Johannes and George another, while Mutti and Vati slept in the third. 'Just till we find a place of our own,' said Vati, trying to find words to thank Frau Marks. But what words could you find for someone who gave you not just a life, but a new life, in a safe country?

Australia had only been bombed a little, in the war, but most of its men and many women had fought, instead of building houses, cars or furniture, so there were not enough houses for everyone to have their own now, nor had houses been repaired or tended much during the war.

George and Mud had worked on Mud's family's farm when her brothers were in the army and her father in the air force. They looked so brown, so tall, impossibly strong. They laughed so easily, and strode along the streets as if there could never be anything around a corner to be afraid of.

Johannes liked them both. They were older, but didn't condescend. They were kind, an understanding kindness, the kindness of people who had known pain and fear too. George didn't even seem to mind a stranger sharing his bedroom, a strange family sharing his home, a family who knew his mother from a time he hadn't shared, and who loved her.

He shared his books too, a whole bookcase of them in the bedroom, another bookcase in the hall, and a bookcase in the living room mostly filled with second-hand paperbacks that Frau Marks had bought. Many of George's books were textbooks, and every book in the house was in English. None had leather covers. But to be in a house where books were loved, where ideas were shared around the table at dinner ... to be in a house, not a barracks. A house ...

The houses all around were shabbier still. 'It is a slum,' said Frau Marks cheerfully. 'There are much better houses in Australia. But this is near the university and it was cheap.' She had made a tiny front garden of bright flowers that bloomed even in the winter, and painted more in a frieze on the fresh white walls of the hall.

The house also had a big dining room, a dim kitchen with old linoleum and a gas stove that spluttered. It had a backyard that was mostly clothes line and baked concrete, with an outdoor toilet and a laundry that smelled of mould and mice, a living room with a bed that was used as a sofa during the day. The elderly couple, whom George called Auntie Thel and Uncle Ron, slept on the sofa when they visited from the country, always bringing two big baskets of jam and fruit and vegetables, butter in glass jars, and a big hunk of sheep meat wrapped in white paper and then brown, as if there was no food to buy in the city.

There was a lot. Australian food had been rationed too, in the war, though there had always been plenty to eat, even if some things were in short supply as so much had to be sent to feed the armies. But now even butter rationing had ended. Roast rabbits even at the railway station, sold by a shabby man in a grey coat and costing only pennies; ham and beef shops where you could buy tasteless sausages and corned beef; butchers with whole windows displaying different cuts of meat, mostly sheep, but some beef and even, sometimes, pork.

Frau Marks served them roast pork with apple sauce on their first night, and they cried together, even George, with Mud hugging Frau Marks fiercely. Mud did many kind things fiercely. She reminded Johannes a little of Helga, though he was not sure why, for Mud was tall and brown and Helga short and fair-skinned, except for her birthmark, and she limped. Helga was quiet and Mud was loud, singing even on the bus, so some passengers frowned but others joined in. '*Click go the shears, boys, click, click, click ...*'

Mud explained the words to him, how shearing sheds worked and Australian elections, and how Australians were the best tennis players in the world and had won almost every sport at the Empire Games, and why Mr Menzies the Prime Minister and everyone else who thought there were reds under the beds were two bob short of a quid, and what 'reds under the beds' and 'two bob short of a quid' meant, and which was the best shop to buy ice cream.

School. A second-hand uniform. A classroom, sitting at ink-stained desks with sludge at the bottom of the ink wells, instead of lessons on the grass or slouching on bunks. One teacher who taught the class everything, instead of many: a teacher who knew less than any of those who had taught him back in the camp, who didn't like a boy who knew about Heisenberg's Uncertainty Principle, when clearly he did not. Boys who called him 'Weedy Weeny' instead of his real name, and 'Swatty Pants' for doing too well in class.

He bore it all, till one day he forgot his lunch and Mud delivered it.

'Hey, Weedy!' yelled one of the tormentors, a boy with green snot in one nostril and scabby knees. 'What have you got for lunch? Reffo cat sausages? Want me to spit in it to make it taste better?'

Mud walked calmly over to the boy who had yelled. Her fist shot out. The boy screamed, holding his bleeding nose.

Mud grabbed Johannes's hand. 'Come on,' she said.

She took him to a milk bar and shouted him a banana split, which was a sliced banana covered with ice cream and then with chocolate sauce and then with nuts and a cherry on top. They discussed Freud and his theories of the subconscious mind as they spooned up ice cream and sauce, and how people who felt insecure were more likely to be the ones who subconsciously feared the stranger, or anyone whom they thought had more than they did, money or intelligence.

'I shouldn't have biffed the kid,' admitted Mud.

'Biffed?'

'Clonked him on the nose like that. It's bad enough that he has to be himself, without me plonking him one.'

It was almost like sitting under the beech trees, talking with Helga. Or rather it was nothing like talking with Helga, who never biffed anyone, but who loved to understand the world as much as he did, and Mud and George.

Would Helga ever have the chance to eat a banana split?

He missed her with an ache that was part fear. She was the only part of the life-within-the-ogre he wished to be reunited with. He had changed. Australia had changed him, as well as the changes that came anyway as you grew and matured.

Helga must be changing too. Could the old Helga-and-Johannes ever exist again?

The next week Johannes went to a smaller school, run by nuns. The nuns didn't know about Heisenberg's Uncertainty Principle either, but they looked interested when he explained it. If kids misbehaved, they lashed them with a cane, on the fingers, but that was right and proper for a teacher when students did not do what they were supposed to do.

Johannes did, and he was happy. Almost happy. And no one called him 'reffo' in the school grounds.

He could not play games, not even cricket — his chest was bad, from being so ill during the war, said Vati, which meant he got out of breath easily. On sports afternoons he stayed in the tiny library, reading. Books were his friends. His only friends, for even if no one called him 'reffo', no one asked him to join their group either.

Weekends were the worst. George and Mud studied, or went to the pictures with their 'mates', which was Australian for 'friend'. Once they asked him to come too, but he felt so out of place, so much younger, and obviously there only because of their kindness, that he refused their later invitations.

Vati worked at a hospital now, not just during the week but on weekends, and Mutti at another hospital for women. Their long days and too-full weeks were partly because Australia did not have enough doctors, so the ones they had needed to work more. But mostly it was because of a thing called 'overtime', which meant that the longer you worked, the more money you received.

'Soon we can rent our own house,' said Vati to Johannes at their early breakfast one Saturday before he and Mutti went to work. He smiled. 'And we have a surprise for you.' He reached under the table, then held out a case to Johannes. A violin case.

Johannes opened it. It *was* a violin, not, say, an unusual container for chocolates or books.

'We have arranged for you to have violin lessons again,' said Mutti, smiling. 'Just like at home.'

Home was not just another land, but another world, a world too frightening to think back to. And, besides, he had never enjoyed playing the violin. He had just been too young to say, 'I'm never going to be good at this.' But the gift of both violin and lessons obviously meant so much to his parents. He almost smiled. Now he was too old to say, 'No. I don't want to.'

Vati handed him a piece of paper with an address written on it. 'Here, at two o'clock this afternoon. The teacher's name is Mr Mittelfeld.' He grinned, as if he was giving Johannes a lifetime ticket to all the banana splits he wanted to eat. 'You must have every advantage. That is why we work so hard.'

'Tennis lessons too, perhaps,' said Mutti blithely.

'No, not tennis,' said Johannes firmly. But he accepted the violin. Perhaps by the end of the year he could find an excuse to give up the lessons.

Mr Mittelfeld's home was part of a bigger house, half an hour's walk from Frau Marks's. A coconut with *No. 5*, the apartment number, written on it sat outside the peeling green door where Johannes knocked.

An old man opened the door. He peered at Johannes through thick glasses.

'Johannes Wolcheki, sir,' said Johannes.

'Ah. Come in. Come in. So, you are a musician.'

'No,' said Johannes. 'I just learned a little, years ago. I haven't played since.'

'But you love music?' The words were strangely intense.

'I don't know,' said Johannes. Something about this crooked man, with his bulging crooked hands, brought forth honesty. He hadn't enjoyed the dances at the camp much, but sometimes he enjoyed listening to the music on Frau Marks's radio.

The old man coughed. 'So. Play.'

Johannes took out the violin, tightened the strings and rubbed resin on the bow as the old man watched. 'You have a good ear,' he said. 'You know how to tune a violin without a tuning whistle. Now play.'

Johannes played. One minute. Two.

'Enough!' The old man held up his deformed hand. 'No, you are no musician.' He looked at Johannes sternly. 'I do not teach for money only. I was once the principal violinist in the Berlin Philharmonic.' His sleeve slid up his arm as he gestured, and Johannes saw the tattoo.

So this is why Mutti and Vati sent me here, he thought. Not just so their son would be properly cultured, but to help a fellow refugee who needed students and fees.

'If I can no longer play for an orchestra, I can teach those who will be great one day. You will not be great. You will not even be good,' the old man said matter-of-factly.

'I'm sorry, sir,' said Johannes. He began to put the violin back in its case, loosening the bow to nestle it in its holder.

'Stop,' said Mr Mittelfeld. He crossed to a frayed floral sofa, a bit like a carpet on legs, and picked up a violin, older than Johannes's, dark wood with a giant scratch in the base. The old man lifted his bow.

It was not music. Or not just music. It was the land beyond the ogre, a place where ogres had no power. Eagles soared and trees sang and wolves forgot to savage, but lifted their noses to the moon to join the song.

At last the old man put down his bow. He looked at Johannes. 'You will never play well,' he said. 'I cannot teach you to play well. But I can teach you music. I will see you next Saturday, at two o'clock.'

'Thank you, sir,' said Johannes. He shook Mr Mittelfeld's hand, waited for him to stop coughing, then said, 'May I bring you some cherry strudel? Frau Marks, who we live with, makes good strudel.'

'I would love cherry strudel,' said Mr Mittelfeld. He smiled and, once again, Johannes felt the ogre did not matter. 'A student brought me a coconut last week. A coconut! And it is warm enough to wear shorts and sandals even in winter. Who could do that in Berlin?' The shabby room with its smell of old cats faded as Mr Mittelfeld added, 'Life is very good.'

Chapter 36

JOHANNES
AUSTRALIA, DECEMBER 1950

How could life be good?

Because the ogre hadn't vanished, even though they had come across the world. Nor had they even reached 'home' yet. They were still travelling, still perched in Frau Marks's house, even if it was a kind house, an ordered house, filled with the scent of apple cake or peach dumplings or veal chops stewed with tomatoes and onion (but no garlic, which Frau Marks said was impossible to buy).

But Helga and Frau Schmidt were still across the ocean, in the land where soldiers of two foreign armies stopped trains, and food was stew with shreds of turnip, and coffee made of acorns, and no milk to make Helga's bones grow big and strong …

He opened the door of Frau Marks's house with his key. 'Hello?' he called, because that was what Mud had said Australians did when they entered a house, though sometimes they called, 'Cooee.'

No answer. Mutti and Vati would still be at work, George and Mud studying or with their friends, Frau Marks at the library, perhaps. It would be St Nicholas's Eve soon, but at the camps few of them had celebrated it. How could St Nicholas come to a DP camp? Even their first Christmas in Australia had just been a church service and handmade presents, his family too bewildered to change such a big custom as Christmas. And did Christmas trees even grow in Australia?

The sun glared onto the concrete gardens, the bitumen road, the roofs that squatted side by side. Christmas did not feel right here, in summer heat ...

He drifted into the kitchen, cut a big hunk of white bread with its cracking black top crust, smeared it with half-melted butter, for the iceman only came once a week to leave a block of ice in the cool safe and it had melted by now, then rummaged for a pot of plum jam. At least Australia had good jam ...

Rat-a-tat-tat! He looked up at the sound of the door knocker. One of George's or Mud's friends, probably — maybe the one who had the record player. He wondered if Mr Mittelfeld had a record player. But perhaps Mr Mittelfeld had symphonies enough in his memory.

He opened the door. 'George isn't —' he began, and stopped.

Helga stood there, with Frau and Herr Schmidt.

Chapter 37

JOHANNES
AUSTRALIA, DECEMBER 1950

'How? When?' He had somehow ushered them into the living room, had even made coffee, real coffee, with Helga's help, and found the apple cake that had been made fresh that morning.

'But I wrote!' said Helga. 'I wrote three times a week!' She looked the same. She looked so different! Taller, her hair cut short and curling, her birthmark faded so it was just the faintest shadow, beautiful in a blue and white dress that looked like it had never been part of another dress, or curtains or a sheet.

'I didn't get any letters!' But they both knew how unreliable mail still was in Germany.

'You wouldn't have got the one saying we were on our way,' said Frau Schmidt. 'It would have travelled on the same ship as us, or even a later one.'

'I wanted to be at the station to meet you!'

'We arrived last night. And slept and slept. And then came here.'

'Where are you staying?'

'A friend rented two rooms for us in his sister's house,' began Herr Schmidt. 'I only reached Sydney yesterday myself ...'

'The rooms are only fifteen minutes' walk from here,' said Frau Schmidt. 'So we can all meet and talk German.'

They had been talking in German, Johannes realised. He hadn't noticed.

'And ... Vati ...' Helga still hesitated before the word, 'has been given a job on a big new building.'

'Not as an engineer yet,' said Herr Schmidt. 'But as an engineer's assistant. A friend and I have begun our own construction company.'

The front door opened. And Frau Schmidt and Frau Marks were in each other's arms, and crying, and Helga and Johannes were somehow in the huddle. And two cups of coffee and the rest of the apple cake later George and Mud arrived, then Mutti and Vati, more hugs and tears and exclamations, and silences that ended with everyone laughing because there was so much that could never be put into words.

'And after all this no homecoming feast,' mourned Frau Marks. 'Only chops for dinner! But I will make pancakes. Pancakes with sour cream — I must use lemons and fresh cream as they have no sour cream here — and plum jam from Mud's mother.'

'My mum makes bonzer plum jam,' said Mud.

'And potato cakes ...'

Johannes expected Helga to go to the kitchen with the women. But she sat on the sofa, so lovely in her blue and white dress, as Vati and Herr Schmidt talked about blocks of land for sale at a place, Killara, where new houses were being built, where they might each build a house; about Johannes's school and how Helga should go there too; about rent prices and what

exams in English involved and how many tonnes their ships had
been …

… and Helga watched him and he watched Helga, and they
smiled.

And it was almost — almost — like they had come home.

Chapter 38

'But the real question is, what would the *reasonable* man say?' pronounced George, sitting with his elbows on the kitchen table with Mud and Johannes and Helga, sounding so like the lawyer he would one day be that Frau Marks wished, desperately, his father could see him. 'That's the foundation of common law. Is it *reasonable* to ban the Communist Party?'

'Reasonable people may not all agree,' argued Johannes earnestly.

'Ha. Where are you going to find a *reasonable* man?' said Mud. 'Blokes aren't reasonable. Ask any woman.'

Helga laughed. It was so good to hear that solemn girl laugh, thought Frau Marks. Sometimes she wondered what Helga had been through. Not a concentration camp, but ... something ... Frau Marks felt Helga kept hidden, perhaps even from her parents. Frau Marks was experienced with secrets. She knew enough to see when others had them too.

Most of her own life was a kind of secret now. She would not burden George with what she had endured in the concentration camp, or had been forced to do there to survive. Neither her son nor his children should ever have to carry memories like that.

Even her life as a happy child and joyous young mother must be cut away. Because in those days she had been German, an enemy, and the enemy had killed the Peaslakes' son, the young man George regarded as an older brother, even though they had never met in person.

The Australians she knew excused her from being German because of her time in the concentration camp, as if the tattoo on her arm divorced her from her country. And yes, perhaps that tattoo meant that for a time her country had renounced her. But she had been happily German, *was* still German, even if she was becoming Australian too, hummed German songs and had to stop herself, longed to recite the German poems that George's father had loved so much, that the child who was now George had once loved too.

She could not. Instead she was grateful that she and her son bore an English surname, so those who met them assumed their background was English, and they now were 'dinkum Aussies, through and through'.

Yet she was happy, she told herself, watching the young people shove their glasses into the sink, listening to the clatter as George and Mud ran upstairs to get their towels and swimming costumes for an afternoon at the beach. She had her house, which she loved, even if ten years ago she would have been shocked at a house so small, in such a poor district, with not even a single servant.

She had friends, not just the Wolchekis and the Schmidts, but Australian women she had met at church, as well as a stubborn old woman down the street who had given her geranium and hydrangea cuttings the first week she had moved here, and then arrived with a plate of hot scones to make sure she had planted them properly.

She and old Mrs O'Connel had shared many scones and memories since then, but Frau Marks had made sure that her conversation never hinted that Germany might be a place of good people, that fascism had been a disease that had infected many nations, and some Australians too. Mrs O'Connel's son and grandson had died in Egypt, fighting Rommel. Frau Marks could not even say that General Rommel had given his own life because he tried to remove Hitler and his madness from his homeland.

Mostly her joy grew from watching George, how every day he grew more to manhood, and not just that, but becoming a man she liked, respected and admired. It was so good to have a son you admired as well as loved. And Mud with her fierce love and laughter was a gift and blessing. She loved Mud like a daughter, and Johannes and Helga too.

No, that wasn't right. She did not love them quite in the way she loved her son. But the love was deep and true.

Yes, she was lucky. Blessed, thought Frau Marks as she automatically began to wash the dishes and plan what to feed the horde for dinner. A roast leg of mutton, perhaps, cooked long and slowly to make it tender, as Thelma Peaslake had shown her, with roast potatoes and roast pumpkin — back home, pumpkin was given only to the pigs, but here it was essential to make the copious gravy Australians, including her son, expected. A plum tart for dessert, using her mother's recipe for almond pastry?

She was happy, Frau Marks repeated to herself as she picked up the tea towel. And if sometimes she felt she bore a wound that she could never quite identify, she managed to ignore it. Surely happiness was enough.

Chapter 39

JOHANNES
AUSTRALIA, 1951

Days had routines now. Routine was good. Routine might not keep soldiers from knocking at the window or prevent the bombs from falling, even atomic bombs like the ones dropped on Japan that the Americans and the Russians threatened each other with now, as if they could not bear to say goodbye to war, but must quickly build another.

But routine meant things mostly happened as expected. Breakfast, walking to school past Helga's house, to walk the rest of the way with her. Sitting with Helga at lunchtime discussing physics, or an interesting article in one of his parents' medical journals, even if the other students thought it strange for a boy and girl to sit together, much less talk about new vaccination techniques.

Helga could not play sport either, because of her limp. But no one teased them. Johannes suspected that one of the nuns had talked to the other students about concentration camps and DP camps and being kind to them, and not mentioning

Helga's birthmark or limp either ... which was ... good ... but embarrassing. And not as good as having friends.

But it had been a long time since he'd had any friends, except for Helga. He thought he had probably forgotten how to make them.

They *had* had Christmas. A strange Australian Christmas, down at Mud's parents' farm, three tables put together and covered with four tablecloths, and straggly home-made decorations and the poorest Christmas tree Johannes had ever seen — not a proper fir tree but one called a she-oak, dropping needles and drooping in the heat, with cotton wool for snow and the decorations mostly kids' drawings, and no candles.

'You'll start a bushfire!' said Mud's mum, shocked, when Johannes suggested candles on the tree. 'I never heard the like!'

No roast pork but two giant hams, with two roast turkeys and three roast chickens, all stuffed with lemon and herb stuffing. No apple sauce but lots of gravy, and plum puddings with cream and custard, which after the shock of strange flavours and textures were delicious, and Christmas cake, which was even better, and beer instead of wine for the men, and carols around the piano, Mud with a voice like a bullfrog but singing anyway, and church that was neither Catholic nor Lutheran but fitted the purpose of the day.

Mud's dad gave Johannes and Helga bicycles — not new ones, of course, for factories weren't making luxuries yet, but old ones repaired and newly painted. They could ride them to school, to libraries further away from home that had more books, even to the beach. Mrs Schmidt made clothes for everyone, out of new cloth now it was no longer rationed, with a sewing machine she had traded for in Italy and carted to Australia; and Mutti and Vati gave books and books and more books; and Helga gave everyone scarves she had knitted; and, even though St Nicholas hadn't come, a man called Santa Claus did, in a rusty ute with Santa in the back, giving bags of what Australians called 'lollies' to everyone, even Mud and George.

Strange shelled creatures called cicadas sang, and even stranger birds called kookaburras laughed, and in the afternoon they flew kites so high and with so much laughter that Johannes thought they must surely be free of the ogre now.

But at night, when dreams ate him, he knew the ogre was still there.

Chapter 40

FRAU MARKS
AUSTRALIA, APRIL 1951

Frau Marks watched Mud flop down in one of the shabby armchairs next to George. 'The whole psychology class had to visit the maternity ward today. There's a woman there who's had twelve children in fifteen years. Twelve! No wonder she has postnatal depression. Plus all of us gawking at her.'

George grinned at her. 'So we're not going to have twelve kids then?'

'Ha,' said Mud. 'Two. If you're lucky, mate.'

Frau Marks looked from George to Mud. They were so young ...

George saw her glance. He leaped up and hugged her, fast and affectionate. 'Don't worry, Mum. I haven't even asked Mud to marry me yet. I'll let you know when I do.'

'I'll let you know when I say yes. *If* I say yes,' said Mud. 'Come on, lazybones,' she added to George, 'I need a swim to wash away the smell of hospital. Do you want to come down to the beach too, Aunt Mutti?'

Aunt Mutti. Auntie Mummy. A strange name, but a strange relationship too. And she liked the sound of it.

Frau Marks shook her head. The two young people would feel they had to stay with her and talk on the beach, instead of surfing. 'I have some work to catch up on.' She had suddenly decided on New Year's Day to do the entrance exam for the university. She was old, of course, older even than her age, after the years of war. But she had a deep feeling it was time for another beginning, a life of her own, not just watching the changing life of her son and his companions. Perhaps university would give it to her.

'I forgot. There's a letter for you,' added George. 'I put it on the kitchen table.' He clattered upstairs to get his swimming costume.

Probably from Gudrun, thought Frau Marks. Gudrun wrote once a month, enclosing a money order, rent for her house. She cashed the money orders, but ripped up the letters without reading them.

Lately the money order had been bigger. She had read the letter that had come with the first larger amount. Her sister had written that they had a house of their own now, that they had arranged for her house to be rented to others at a higher rent, and that she would make sure they took good care of it. That once again she was sorry …

Frau Marks had thrown the letter away.

This letter lay on the table. Strange, how a small piece of paper could carry so much emotion across the world. She looked at it more closely. The writing was not Gudrun's.

Had something happened to her sister? For the first time a small prickle of what she had once felt for Gudrun broke through the wall she had built so carefully in her mind. She picked up the envelope and opened it.

Dear Frau Marks,

I write to you with sad news, and with glad. My aunt, whom you knew as Sister Columba, died two weeks ago, the day after we had news through the Red Cross that you had survived, and somehow made your way to Australia to be united with your son.

Guilt froze her fingers, so the letter almost dropped from her hand. Sister Columba had survived! Had been alive for more than six years since she had seen her. How long had she been helpless, in the travesty of a post-war hospital? And now she had died. Shock warred with guilt, grief and joy.

As soon as she had gone to London, she had asked Miriam to use her contacts to try to find Sister Columba, but she had not been listed in any of the DP camps or by the Red Cross. Frau Marks had assumed that her friend had died. She had seemed so very close to death the day she and Dr Wolcheki had been forced to leave the camp.

I should have looked harder, she thought. Looked again! For sometimes it took years for people to get the precious papers that gave them a legal, registered existence. But she had not known that then.

Frau Marks forced herself to keep reading.

My aunt was unable to speak towards the end, but she smiled when I told her you had been found, and pressed my hand, so I am sure she understood. She remained weak in body ever since the war, cared for at the Mother House, but strong in spirit and in love. She often spoke of you when she was stronger, and it was her dearest wish that you should be happy and your life be filled with love. Perhaps she refused to die until she knew that you were safe.

Although we have never met, I feel I know you, from the stories of my aunt, as she felt she knew your son from the stories you told her of him. If you are able, it would mean so much to me to know what your life is now. Perhaps I could leave that letter on my aunt's grave, with the flowers we take to her each week. It is strange, but each time I do so I know I should cry, but instead I feel joy. The sky is always just a little brighter when I think of my aunt, whose prayers were so often for you, as mine are for you too.

Yours,
Frau Clementine

She sat at the kitchen table, and she cried. She who had not cried for so long, because there comes a time when there are not tears enough to be shed, sobbed now.

She had thought she had become a woman of love when she found her George. She had been wrong. It took Sister Columba to show her how.

She found paper, a pen, ink, managed to stop her hands trembling as she wrote:

My dear Gudrun,

Thank you for the letters, for the rent for the house and for all the care you take of my property now.

I am sorry for all the letters I have not answered, for all I have not said, for all the years of sisterhood I have not given.

I understand. You loved your family, and could not risk them. You loved your country, and so its enemies had to be yours. Please forgive the hardness of my heart that has kept us apart these last years.

I do not think I can ever return to visit Germany. You might find Australia rough and a little uncultured, but it is also beautiful and kind. Your children would love its beaches. I hope, one day, you might visit us here, that our children may meet and know their cousins and that we can embrace again, as sisters.

With love, always,
Marlene

Chapter 41

JOHANNES
AUSTRALIA, JUNE 1951

'What do *you* want to do?' asked Johannes. He and Helga had caught a bus to the Botanic Garden by the harbour before his violin lesson, to watch the ships come in, the seagulls flash above the water, to sit on the short grass and talk.

He had discovered the Botanic Garden when Mr Mittelfeld took his favourite students to the Conservatorium of Music, which perched on the hill next to the garden. They had been to three concerts and an opera now, and every time the music left him soaring like the seagulls. Sometimes he found his face damp with tears too, which would have been embarrassing, if the others had not sometimes cried as well, and even Mr Mittelfeld.

'All strong emotion can bring tears,' explained Mr Mittelfeld. 'Why should they be given only to sadness? The greatest applause a musician can have is that moment's silence, when the audience must brush away their tears before they clap.'

It had made him wish, just for a moment, that he could be a professional musician, like Tom or Harriet planned to be, and possibly the others too.

The kids at school had been discussing what they'd do after the Intermediate too. Some would leave school, but neither his parents nor the Schmidts would allow that, even if Helga and Johannes had wanted to. This was a new land, with opportunity, and they must take every opportunity it offered. The blocks of land had been purchased, although no houses stood on them yet.

'I want to become a doctor,' said Helga, with no hesitation.

'Why?' Helga had joined the Junior Red Cross, and wore a white dress with a red cape and black shoes to school every Wednesday. And on Saturday afternoons when he went to his music lessons with Mr Mittelfeld, she visited hospitals with the other Red Cross girls, handing out posies of flowers wrapped in carefully cut doilies, or facecloths they had hemmed and filled with bath salts or sweet soap they'd bought with money raised by toffee days at school.

They learned first aid at the Red Cross, but Johannes didn't think Helga had joined for that, nor to make friends, though it had helped. The other girls asked her to their birthday parties now.

He had even made friends himself, with two boys who liked physics and electronics as much as he did. They were saving up to buy the parts to make a wireless set each, like the model in *Popular Mechanics*.

'Doctors help people,' said Helga simply.

'I want to be a doctor too.' It was the first time he had admitted it. So boring, to take up the same profession as your parents. But bodies fascinated him. Not just bodies, but how parts of the body fitted together, like molecules and microbes. 'I'd like to specialise in skin diseases.'

'I want to go into research, find a cure for a big disease. Something that will save millions of people. Six million. Forty million!' Her voice was filled with a strange earnestness.

'You'd be stuck inside a laboratory all day with test tubes. Wouldn't you rather work with people?'

'I ... I'd rather work with children. A paediatrician. But research would be more valuable.'

Johannes had a sudden vision of a thousand children, stumbling in the snow, of small frozen bodies, of every child dead, except for him, as Nurse Stöhlich carried him back to the camp hospital. He had never told Helga about that march, nor had his mother or Frau Marks ever spoken of it to him.

He forced himself back to the present. 'Fair enough.' It was an Australian phrase. He was getting good at using Australian expressions now, carefully inserting them wherever he could. He was glad that Helga wanted to do medicine too. It meant that they'd keep studying together.

He stood. 'How about an ice cream?' He was not just speaking English now, but Australian English. No one hearing him speak would yell, 'Reffo!' these days.

'Sounds good,' said Helga, in Australian too. The ice-cream van sat at the top of the garden, outside the Conservatorium of Music. Mr Mittelfeld was going to take his students to the Conservatorium again in a few weeks, to hear a famous visiting violinist. Johannes wondered if he might bring Helga too. She did not play the violin, but Mr Mittelfeld taught him because he loved music, not because he was good at playing it. That love had deepened with every lesson, every concert, every ABC orchestra performance he heard on the wireless, seeping into his soul, even licking at the coals of hate and fear, the hellfire that was always lurking when you still lived in the ogre's belly.

But it was easier to forget the ogre for a while today, with an ice cream in his hand, a double header, and Helga pretty in her flowered dress licking hers beside him. He only noticed her birthmark now when someone commented on it, asking with sympathy if she'd been burned. Frau Marks had offered to cover it with make-up, but for some reason Helga had refused.

Johannes was glad. The make-up might have stopped the awkward questions, but he didn't want a different Helga. He never would.

They caught the bus back, in time for Helga to change into her Red Cross uniform, and for him to wrap Frau Marks's almond biscuits in greaseproof paper for Mr Mittelfeld. The biscuits were a gift of love, a gift of thanks. Money was not enough for what Mr Mittelfeld gave his students.

He walked along the streets, carrying his violin case in one hand, the biscuits in the other, then knocked on the door. The coconut was still there, still with *No. 5* painted on it.

No answer. He knocked again. This time the door opposite opened. An elderly woman stuck her head out. 'Are you one of the old man's students? He's in the hospital.'

'What's wrong?' he asked in alarm.

'It's his lungs, they say. I went to sit with him yesterday and he did look bad. So sad, isn't it?'

'Which hospital? Please.'

He didn't walk. He ran. When you had known the camps, you knew how quickly a life could end.

But not Mr Mittelfeld's life. He had only just been given a new one! He deserved more time. Much more time, to enjoy it, to eat the cakes and biscuits his students gave him, and the coconuts, to see his best students become famous musicians and play in concert halls around the world ...

He reached the hospital.

Chapter 42

JOHANNES
AUSTRALIA, JUNE 1951

Mr Mittelfeld lay in a small white-painted room, between white sheets, his white face on a white pillow, his sparse hair grey. Green curtains had been pulled around the bed of the only other occupant.

This is where people die, thought Johannes.

Mr Mittelfeld's eyes were shut. He breathed as if a machine pulled the air in and out of his lungs, as if it needed a massive engine to do that simple thing. But there was no engine, only the frail body on the bed.

How had Mr Mittelfeld become so much smaller in the past week? Johannes sat, the paper bag of biscuits in his hand. Stupid biscuits, because Mr Mittelfeld could not eat them. But it hadn't seemed right to leave them back at his apartment, or throw them away.

The eyes opened. Mr Mittelfeld smiled.

'I ... I hope you're feeling better, sir.'

'Yes.' The word was a harsh whisper between two gasps of breath.

Relief flowed through him. 'I'm glad. I was afraid ...'

'That ... I ... would die? Of course ... I am ... dying.' The smile again. 'I have seen enough of death ... to know its ... face.'

'No! It's not fair!'

A faint shrug. 'Who said that life was f ... fair? Humans ... invented ... fair. *We* must be ... fair. But ... life? Not so.'

'Then God isn't fair!'

'What ... religion ... says ... He is? But He ... gave us ... ways ... to bear what isn't ... fair. To ... to make ... life ... good.'

'You made life good for me, sir. You gave me music.'

'I ... know. That gave me ... much joy. My violin ... I wish ... it to be yours.'

'But I'm your worst student! I'm not a good musician!'

A cough cracked his laugh. 'You are not a ... good musician. But it is not ... a good violin. How could a ... refugee teacher ... afford ... a good ... violin?'

'But it sounds beautiful when you play it, sir.' Anguish ran through him like a lightning strike. Would he never hear that music again?

'That is because you ... listen for the beauty. That is ... important, Kindchen. Listen. Always listen ... for the beauty. It is always ... there.'

'Not always.'

'You do not search ... hard ... enough.' The coughing laugh spluttered again. It went on until a nurse arrived and held water to the old man's lips.

'Perhaps it's time for your visitor to go now.'

Mr Mittelfeld smiled at her. 'It is soon ... time for me ... to go too, eh? Let the boy stay.'

The nurse hesitated. She was young, so very starched and black-stockinged. She touched the old man's thin shoulder in its pyjama top lightly. 'I'll pull the curtains so Matron doesn't see.'

Mr Mittelfeld waited, wheezing, until the curtains were drawn. 'Even in … the camps, there was … beauty. Did you never look up … at the sky, or hear … a lark sing?'

'No,' said Johannes. Why would you look at the sky and listen to birdsong when you were in the belly of the ogre?

'But they were there,' whispered Mr Mittelfeld. 'And you are here. So much … joy … that you … are here. A gift to know … I gave you … beauty.' The voice faded. The breathing grew louder, in and out, and in and out. His eyes shut again. But his hand moved, out of the tidy sheets, towards Johannes.

Johannes took his hand. A papery hand. A winter leaf. Tattered, scarred, splotched with red scars and brown spots. A cold hand, for a man of so much warmth.

Mr Mittelfeld breathed. In. Out. In. Out.

The nurse peered in, then went away.

In. Out. In. Out.

Another nurse. 'Are you all right?' she asked softly.

Was he? Johannes didn't know. He nodded anyway.

In. Out. In. Out.

Silence.

He should call the nurse. Call a doctor. A normal boy would call someone.

A normal boy did not know death as Johannes did.

Mr Mittelfeld's face looked faintly grey, more sunken … Johannes hesitated, then stood stiffly and kissed the cold cheek. 'I love you,' he whispered. 'I am glad you didn't die alone.'

He opened one of the curtains a little bit, and left it open, so the nurse could see he had gone. That both of them were gone. He walked out of the hospital.

Chapter 43

JOHANNES
AUSTRALIA, JUNE 1951

He didn't know where he was going till he reached the house where the Schmidts rented their rooms. He needed Helga. Always, when life was hard. He went round to the back door and looked in and there she was, doing her homework at the table in the otherwise empty kitchen.

He said, 'Helga,' and then said nothing, because his voice was gone. He suddenly realised she should be at her Red Cross meeting. 'Why are you here?' he managed.

'Mrs Robinson's sick. What's wrong?' She stood, crossed the room, then took his hand and led him to the table. She reached automatically into the cupboard for the cocoa, then into the cold chest for the milk, and poured it into a saucepan.

Johannes said, 'Mr Mittelfeld is dead. Pneumonia. He left me his violin.' And music, he thought. And the knowledge that all those years in the camps the sky was beautiful and a lark sang, but I didn't know to look or listen.

'I'm sorry,' said Helga gently. She put the cocoa in front of him, sat opposite him, watched him sip. Sweet and milky, as cocoa had never been until they came here. He sipped again, trying to work out what he felt. And then he knew.

'I hate him,' he said quietly. 'Almost all I am is hating him.'

'Mr Mittelfeld?' asked Helga, startled.

'No! *Hitler!* He stole Mr Mittelfeld's life. He stole it twice! Once in the camp, and now here — Mr Mittelfeld should have had years of life here. Being happy. But because of the camps, because of Hitler, his lungs were scarred and so he died. I wish … I wish he hadn't died.'

'Mr Mittelfeld?' Helga looked confused.

'*Hitler!* I want to tear him into pieces — small pieces, over a long time. Make him feel the agony as well. Millions of agonies, every single torment that he caused. It was Hitler. All him! Like Nurse Stöhlich said,' Johannes didn't even realise he had used her old name, 'Hitler was a bacterium that infected all of Europe. Destroyed most of Europe! One man infected them all! But he cannot pay because he is dead. He cannot feel the anguish. Mr Mittelfeld was left to hurt, to die, but Hitler is safe and dead and can never feel pain or suffer loss …'

It was as if coals that smouldered had at last burst into flame. His whole body ached with anger. 'Every night, the nightmares come. Every night! Every time I see barbed wire, I remember what it was like to be behind it. Hitler killed us. He killed us all! Even now, while we are still alive, he kills us still!' When had his voice risen to a scream?

And then he stopped. Because Helga should be comforting him. Helga should hold his hand. Helga always helped. But Helga only sat there on the kitchen chair, cold and far away.

'Helga?' he said.

She said quietly, 'Hurt me then.'

'You?'

'You want to hurt Hitler? Make him pay? Then hurt me!'

'But you …' he almost said 'I love you', 'you are my friend.'

'I am Hitler's daughter,' said Helga flatly.

He stared. Was she joking? But her face was twisted. And he knew: it was the truth. This was what Helga had been hiding. This was what drove her to give comfort in the camp hospitals, even with chamberpots and pus-filled wounds, to feel that she must save six million people, or forty million, with medical research.

Helga, who was not a Schmidt, who must have been adopted only in the last days of the war, he thought, remembering conversations from back then, just after he met her. And yet …

'Hitler didn't have a daughter,' he said.

'He did.' Helga's voice was still small and flat. 'He had me. But I am small, not tall and blonde. I am crippled. Ugly. Marred. He could not say to Germany, "This is my daughter." He was *ashamed*.'

Johannes said nothing. His mind had turned to stone. This was too heavy to take in.

'Well?' Helga picked up a fruit knife lying on the table, offered it to him. 'Do you want to slice me up instead of him?'

'No, of course —'

'Because you should! What did you say? All of Europe was infected? Well, it was. And I am Hitler's daughter and I am all that's left.' Tears ran down her face now and mucus from her nose. 'All these years, people saying, "So good is Helga Schmidt." They don't know that I am the worst person in the world.'

'But how did you …? Why didn't you …?'

'Why didn't I stop him? Because I didn't know what he was doing! There in the centre of it all, they only told me that Duffi was wonderful. They wouldn't let me call him Vati, so I called him Duffi. Duffi was the hero who had saved our country when the French occupied us and made Germany starved and poor. I didn't know! And then when I began to understand, what could I do? I only saw him twice in the last three years of the war, just for a few minutes. What can a child do? Even if I had the chance to talk to him, what could I have said? Do not kill millions of people, Duffi. I … I will sulk or kick you if you do. But I did nothing. Nothing! And now I never can!'

Helga's face was serious. She really was … Johannes could not even think the name, the hated name, nor put that name with Helga's. And yet …

'Helga Hitler,' he whispered.

'Heidi Hitler,' she said. 'That is who I am.' The loathing in her voice was even more intense than his. 'A soldier took me from the bunker, near the end. A bomb killed him before he could get me to whatever safety they had arranged. And there I was, alone in the rubble of Berlin, no longer Heidi Hitler, and I found the Schmidts.

'Frau Schmidt needed help, and I could give it. Her daughter, Helga, had just been killed, by the Russians. Frau Schmidt only just survived. So I helped her, and used Helga's papers, and Frau Schmidt was grateful and called me her daughter, then Hannes was killed, and I was all she had left. And Herr Schmidt accepted me out of gratitude, thinking I had saved his wife, not knowing who I really was, that it was all a lie, and it was they who'd saved me.

'It is all pretend, always has been. I am not good! I am bad, evil. I must be evil, like my father, so any good I do must be false, a pretence so people like me. Everything! I was born rotten …' She was weeping now.

She stood. 'And now you know my secret, and Mutti and Vati ... the Schmidts ... they will know, and Frau Marks and George and Mud and everyone, and they will hate me because they *should* hate me. I hate myself. I hate myself!'

Then she was gone, out the back door, down the steps. He heard her footsteps and her sobs.

Chapter 44

JOHANNES
AUSTRALIA, JUNE 1951

He knocked the chair over as he ran after her, but she had vanished by the time he reached the street. He looked to the right, and then the left, and saw her running, the strangely bouncing run because of her limp.

He ran too, but not fast. Because he must give her time to stop crying, to stop running, so they could talk. About what …

He didn't know. Just talk. Think.

She was Hitler's daughter. Heidi Hitler. All his hatred had only one place to go. To her. To Helga. Because she was Helga, not Heidi, had been Helga for six years.

'Helga!' he called. 'Helga!'

She didn't answer. Just kept running, towards the main road. No!

He ran faster, but she reached the main road before he did. His lungs screamed. He hesitated as a truck thundered around a corner. He saw Helga stare at the truck. He saw her calculate.

He pushed his body one last time. He leaped, as the teachers had shown him how to do when they thought he might be able to play football. He reached her just in time to see the driver's face, startled and then terrified, as he swerved his big truck across the road, missing an oncoming car by inches, then thundered on, as Helga lay on the road underneath him, sobbing, clutching at the tarmac as if to claw her way back to the middle of the road and its traffic.

Another car swerved around them. The car stopped. A man called out, 'You kids all right?'

No, thought Johannes. We are the most not-all-right people in the world. But he stood. He put his hand down to Helga and helped her up as yet another car swerved, stepped back onto the verge and called, 'Thank you. Just an accident!' then waited till the man drove away.

He looked at Helga.

'Helga,' he said.

'No! Heidi.'

'Heidi. Helga. You are the best person I know.'

'But don't you see? What if ... what if Duffi was trying to be good too?'

Johannes thought of that small man. Small, like Helga was small, dark-haired like her. He remembered him standing on the balcony, screaming in fury, soaking in ten thousand angry cheers.

Helga was not that. Helga was small and good.

Helga was love. Not hate.

So that was what he said. 'You are not him. If you are a ... a bacterium, you spread love, not hate. That is who you are, Helga or Heidi. You are love.'

She collapsed into a ragged heap on the rough grass of the road verge, onto a pulped-up cigarette packet littering the ground. She said, 'I … I have never known what I am. I have tried to be good. But all the time I lived a lie. Don't you see? If Mutti and Vati, the Schmidts, had known who I was, they would not have kept me. Never loved me. You would not have been my friend.'

He considered that. At last he nodded. 'No. You're right — I wouldn't have been your friend. Not then. But now I am.'

'Even though I am Heidi? Hitler's daughter?'

'You are you.' He hesitated because, unless this wasn't life and death it was too embarrassing to say, and then realised it *was* life and death, and so he said, 'I love you. Really love you. I always will. I love you not just because you are good and have always helped me. I love you not because you are Helga or Heidi or any name. But because you are you.' He put his arm out tentatively, not sure how you hugged a girl, then found her in his arms.

Drivers stared as they passed. It didn't matter. They sat there, on the grubby verge.

At last she whispered, 'I have to tell Mutti and Vati. Tell everyone.'

'No.'

'They should know the truth!'

'The truth would only hurt them. They have been hurt too much.'

'They have been hurt too much to have more lies from me.'

He considered that. Finally he said, 'We'll ask Frau Marks.' For Frau Marks was the wisest person he knew, now Mr Mittelfeld was dead. And like Mr Mittelfeld, Frau Marks had also been eaten by the ogre. His parents were wise about medicine and building houses, but somehow Frau Marks knew more about people. And his parents would be too tired when they came home from the hospitals to cope with the shock of knowing Hitler's daughter, or think what they should say to her. 'We can trust Frau Marks.'

He felt Helga nod against his shoulder.

—◈—

They walked hand in hand. It was embarrassing again, a bit, and wonderful, a bit more, and neither mattered because today he had almost lost Helga and now he would not let her go.

Would Frau Marks be home?

She was, kneeling in the tiny front garden, planting a row of flowers in well-dug soil. She glanced up at them, then stared. 'Helga! You've hurt your knee! Johannes, your elbow ...'

We must have grazed ourselves on the road, thought Johannes. He hadn't noticed the dirt and blood. 'It's fine,' he began.

'It is not fine. Come inside. Let's clean them up before they get infected.'

They followed her, still hand in hand. It would be easier to talk inside. George and Mud were not there, Johannes saw with relief. Frau Marks poured disinfectant onto some cotton wool. 'This will sting.'

It did. He didn't mind the pain. But the smell brought back the stench of death within the ogre's belly, and that was hard to bear.

Helga's hand was warm in his, though, and suddenly the memory of the war vanished and all the world was Helga and Frau Marks, the scent of almond biscuits cooling on the bench and, yes, the sky outside was a high wide blue, and beautiful, and that was a magpie singing, not a lark, and the light streaming through the window was pure gold. Why had he never seen the beauty of Australian light before?

'Helga? Johannes?' asked Frau Marks, looking at him with the concern she had put aside to tend their grazes. 'Was ist los?'

So Helga told her. Told her about a childhood in a house high on a mountain, where sometimes a man called Duffi visited; where she watched hedgehogs and studied with Fräulein Gelber; about the farmhouse they lived in later with Frau Leib; the visit from the Führer when she wore her best shoes; the bunker where she called Hitler 'Vati' for the only time and he said, 'Who is this girl?' and the soldier took her to safety; but there was no safety, for he was killed, and then she found Frau Schmidt and Hannes, and then Johannes …

'And finally we came to the camp and met you,' said Helga. Johannes still held her hand tightly, not because he was scared for her now, but so she would know she was Helga, not Heidi. Helga!

'I knew that nothing I could ever do would make up for what my father did, for who I am, but still I had to try.' The tears fell again now. She brushed them away angrily. 'I have always known that if Mutti and Vati knew who I was, if you did, if Johannes did or his parents, that you would all hate me. Everyone must hate me, because I am Hitler's daughter. I am all there is left to hate.'

'No,' said Frau Marks calmly, 'you are not.' She crossed to the fridge. For a moment Johannes thought she was going to make them cocoa. He wouldn't be able to stand the memories if she made them cocoa now. But instead she brought out a squat bottle of lemonade, frost clouding the glass, then fetched two glasses from the sideboard, two special glasses with coloured bands around the base that were only used for special drinks like lemonade or sarsaparilla, and filled them and passed one to each of them. 'You are not Hitler's daughter.'

'You think I am making up a sick fantasy?' demanded Helga, suddenly fierce.

'No. I think all you say happened is true. But no one ever told you that you were Hitler's daughter, did they? The only time you called him "Father" he denied you?'

'He said that so that I could escape,' said Helga stiffly. 'Because he loved me ...'

'How many times had you met him?' The voice was still soft.

Helga considered. 'Twenty, perhaps. He brought me presents, when I was very young, before the war became so bad. A doll with yellow hair and blue eyes. Perfect, as I was not.'

'And your papers? What name was on your papers?'

'I ... I don't know. I never saw my papers. Fräulein Gelber must have had them. Given them to the soldier who was killed.'

'Helga, Heidi ... which name do you prefer?'

'Helga,' said Helga.

'Helga, Hitler had no children.'

'I told you, he was ashamed of me ...'

'You have told me that you think he was ashamed of you, of your lack of perfection. Hitler was the most important man in Germany, in Europe. Do you think he could ever have had a child and no one knew? He wasn't able to have children. But he *did* have foster children. A patient in the hospital I worked in, during the war, told me about it. Her husband worked in the propaganda office, with Herr Goebbels.' Frau Marks met Helga's eyes. 'Children Hitler adopted only for propaganda purposes. He was the Father of Germany — Goebbels advised him that people must see him as a father of German children too.'

Helga sat very still. At last she said, 'He would have adopted children with blonde hair and blue eyes. Perfect children. Not one like me.'

'Some of the children were the orphans of soldiers who had fought with him in the Great War, though your parents must have died much later, of influenza perhaps, or an accident. I don't think there is any way we could ever know. Perhaps,' said Frau Marks carefully, 'your limp, your birthmark, was why no one took pictures of you with the Führer, as they did of him with the other foster children.'

Helga sat as if words had been leached out of her, like colour from litmus paper when you left it soaking for too long.

Johannes said to crack the silence, 'What happened to the other foster children?' Others, he thought. I believe what Frau Marks says is true. Helga is not Hitler's daughter. She is ...

Helga. The person she had always been. Herself. No more nor less.

'I think the other foster children must have been taken to safety, in secrecy, like you were supposed to be,' said Frau Marks quietly. 'I remember pages of people with the surname Hitler in the Berlin phone book before the war. Now, they say, there are none. The name has vanished. But those children, like you, like those other Hitlers who have changed their names, would be innocent.' Frau Marks smiled at them sadly. 'But even if you had been Hitler's daughter, why should you be guilty for what Hitler did? If you found out that Johannes's father had done something wrong — and I am sure he has not, but just suppose — would you think it was Johannes's fault?'

'No!'

'So why should it be different for you?'

'Because ... because the evil was so big. The hate is so big.'

'Ah, hate,' said Frau Marks. 'You said there was no one left to hate. But there are many, many who are still being tried for war crimes. It will go on, perhaps, till the last one is dead. There is hate for all the people who looked away, who saw but would not see, who did not want to see, but kept their lives nice. People like my sister, who blamed me for bringing a crumb of the *unpleasantness* into her tidy life. And I hated her for that too.'

'You mean you don't now?' asked Johannes.

'I saw my son,' said Frau Marks quietly. 'I thought, I am a mother again. And in that moment Sister Columba's words came back to me. Will you be a woman of love or hate? So I pushed the hate aside, to make room for love.'

'Just like that?' whispered Helga.

'No. Not just like that. It took work. And years. All my life, perhaps, I will have to wake up and decide: today I will not be filled with hate. Anger still keeps breaking through. But I keep trying to understand. Understand my sister's small and frightened life, trying to be nice in a mad world. Trying even to understand Hitler, that small, angry man, changing the map of Europe, soaking in the cheers, but never happy. Never fulfilled, as I am happy and fulfilled, with my family, my house in the sunlight, my memories, my friends. I had to forgive, not for my sister's sake, but for mine. For George's sake, so he has a mother who is not made of bitterness. For his future children, if he has them. To stop the passing on of hate. Once you realise that hate is like bacteria infecting others, you know you have to stop it. I won't pass hate onto my grandchildren. But if I can, I will pass on love.'

Silence dripped in long slow seconds. Johannes was aware of Helga's hand still in his, the tears drying now on her face. 'Helga,' he whispered. 'Are you all right?'

She nodded.

'Frau Marks? Should we tell Helga's parents? My parents?'

'I will tell them,' said Frau Marks gently. 'But no one else. Because Helga was also right when she kept her secret. When lives have been hacked away till all that is left is hate, there will be many who want to fling that hate at whoever they can find. Even a child who was Hitler's foster daughter.'

They drank the lemonade. They ate the almond biscuits, and phoned the Schmidts to explain Helga was visiting Frau Marks and not to worry if she was late home.

And then they walked, not to go anywhere in particular, but just to walk together, still hand in hand as Frau Marks waved to them from her gate, the flowers bright behind her.

The sky stretched like a blue balloon. The clouds bobbed like ducks upon a lake. The light poured into the world in a golden stream, even here in this street of shabby houses, and a magpie sang again. Johannes loved them all. He loved Frau Marks too. He loved music, his parents, Mr Mittelfeld, and he would love the old man's violin. And mostly, he loved Helga.

I am a man of love, he thought. This afternoon, probably, perhaps, hate might seep back in. Hate will nibble at my soul at four in the morning, with memories that wake me screaming. Hate will try to flood me when I see the newsreels at the movie theatres and they show Hitler once again. But I have defeated him at last.

I am no longer in the belly of the ogre.

Goodbye, Mr Hitler. You are no longer part of me.

Chapter 45

JOHANNES
AUSTRALIA, 1972

On the corner by the park lives a house of love and stories.

A cat called Fuzzball lives there too. She twines about the legs of the children, but sometimes she sits by the window and watches the pigeons and sighs.

The neighbours call it 'the doctors' house' for on the ground floor of the house are the surgery and waiting rooms where the mother and father see their patients. The father, whose name is Johannes, is a doctor for people's minds. The mother's name is Helga and she heals the pain of children.

Sometimes in the night a patient rings the bell to say a doctor is needed urgently. But mostly, at night, there are hugs and stories for Christine and for Gregory in the bedrooms that look out onto the trees.

The night-time stories are adventures, of flying in a rainbow boat to the land of silver dragons, where houses sit in crags above sheer cliffs and the snow tastes of ice cream and the trees are loaves of fruit bread.

Sometimes, in the holidays, when they meet their friends for picnics, the adults and the children sit on blankets on the ground.

They tell different stories now the children are old enough to understand them.

George tells the story of the night he almost killed a helpless enemy, then realised in the darkness that hatred is contagious. Hatred has power. But love has power too, and that night he helped the man live.

And Mud, who is his wife, laughs and says it was a good thing that he did, for the man was not an enemy but Charlie Lee, who is their son's Godfather now.

The other Mrs Marks, who is older, tells the story of Sister Columba, who gave her a talisman to keep her safe, not on her body but in her heart. Mrs Marks cups her hands, then opens them and, for a second, the children can almost see the word shining in the shadows. *Love.*

Helga tells of Frau Leib, and the day her pig followed her into her bedroom and began to eat the quilt.

Johannes tells of a man called Opa, who said that 'Words kept in the heart cannot be burned', and how a line of ragged children died in the snow, but how he lived because a nurse carried him, a nurse whose arms were warm, despite the cold.

The stories make them cry, sometimes, but they are healing tears. They teach us to remember to see the beauty in the world, the glint of sunlight on the leaves, the taste of cherry strudel, to face the horror and the hatred but to hold them at arm's length, so we can see the love and beauty all around. What we choose to see is what we are.

When you know how to hold the bad things of the world, you do not need to look away. And Mrs Marks smiles and says, 'Sister Columba told me that every day we must open our eyes to one wrong thing and say aloud, to ourselves and others, "This is not right."'

I am Johannes. I am a man of love, not hate. I love my wife, my children, my friends, my patients. I feel the love spread from my hands across the world, to join the hands of others.

I tell the story of the ogre too, the one called Mr Hitler.

There in the park, with my family and my friends, the ogre is dead at last, for me, for Frau Marks, and for Helga. But others have had to carry him in their hearts all their lives. When an ogre swallows you, it is not easy to be free.

The world has many ogres. Some, like Mr Hitler, do not even know that they are ogres, but dream they are the hero of the story.

But I have learned this in the years since I was ten years old: when you see injustice, stand beside each other and seize your spears. My spears are made of words. Yours may be different. But do not hesitate or look away. If too many look away, the ogres win. To be mostly deeply human we must risk our lives for others. Only when we stand together can we be truly free.

It is not easy fighting ogres. No one who fights an ogre comes away unscarred, even if you cannot see the wounds. And so you owe the ogre hunters this.

When the ogre has been vanquished, sit down upon the quiet earth and try to understand the ogre's anguish and his twisted fear. Only by understanding can we stop them rising in our midst.

When you understand, forgive.

And then stand up, and live.

Live well.

Author's Note

This book, like *Hitler's Daughter* and *Pennies for Hitler*, is based on real events and people. The stories behind the books can be found at jackiefrench.com. *Goodbye, Mr Hitler*, like the others, is fiction, but historical fiction should weave between the facts, and not contradict anything that actually happened.

This history in *Goodbye, Mr Hitler* is as accurate as I am able to recreate, but the details of Johannes's short time in Auschwitz may conflict with other accounts. The concentration camp's procedures of even a few weeks before had changed greatly by December 1944, and seem to have been far more disorganised with the Russian army so close, and Germany so desperate, which is one of the reasons I had Johannes arrive at that time. But no two accounts I have been able to find accord exactly. The camp was enormous. Routines changed often over the years. The other reason, of course, for having the main characters arrive so close to the camp's liberation was so that they had a chance to survive.

The two refugee camps and the voyages bringing displaced persons to Australia in this book are also based on real ones, but I have not given names or locations as it is impossible to find enough detail to be sure no inaccuracy crept in.

There *will* be inaccuracies in this book. The war, and its aftermath, are too large and complex to be entirely understood by one historian, or even hundreds or thousands trying to recreate those days. But the most important words in this book are those spoken to me by those who were there: who survived, who hated ... but who had the strength and courage to give the world extraordinary gifts of love.

Acknowledgements

Of all the books I have written, this is the most important. It is also the one that belongs least to me.

The book's theme that forgiveness is necessary both personally and for the good of the world was inspired by the Holocaust survivor volunteers at the Sydney Jewish Museum.

On my first visit to the museum I heard Holocaust survivor Olga Horak speak to a packed auditorium of teenagers, quietly detailing her own story that is not mine to tell. To quote one young man who heard her, 'I knew about the Holocaust, but I didn't understand. I just didn't know.'

Olga's story of hatred and privation was harrowing, and yet she spoke gently and, to the young people there, with love. It was one of the greatest privileges of my life to listen to her and yet, back then, I could not have articulated why.

Years later, as I continued to make an annual visit to the museum, I was told quietly by a staff member of the enormous personal tragedy Olga had just suffered. Yet she still arrived, as scheduled, to speak. Later, I tried clumsily to express my sympathy to her. She took my hand and said, 'Without this place I could not keep going.'

Olga showed me that doing good for others can save your life.

I already knew I must write a sequel to *Hitler's Daughter*. After thousands of letters and emails asking me if Heidi in the book really was Hitler's daughter, I needed to explicitly explain that Heidi would have been one of the foster children adopted for propaganda purposes, even if she hoped desperately that she really was the daughter of Germany's leader. The story of Georg's mother, from *Pennies for Hitler*, was still to be told too.

But this book also began far earlier, when as a teenager I asked my English teacher, 'Why?' Why did the world look away from the Holocaust? Why were Jewish people — or even those whose distant ancestors were Jewish — targeted?

Gillian Pauli was an inspired teacher, of deep and profound compassion. (She is still a woman of deep and profound compassion, though no longer, formally, a teacher.) She brought me armfuls of books every Monday, at a time when I needed those books to survive the horror I had learned not to even try to talk about at school.

I thought the books were from her recent stint at university. I found out years later that she had hunted them out for me, the books I needed to understand the world, to give me the hope and courage to keep going.

Gillian Pauli lent me *The Protocols of the Elders of Zion*, an 1890s book of vicious anti-Semitic propaganda, to show me how lies can be used to create fear and hatred. She told me, a long time later, how she had to convince the shop where she bought it that it was for research, not because she was a Nazi sympathiser or an anti-Semite.

A friend of hers, who had survived Dachau, saw it on her kitchen table.

'Why do you have this book?' he demanded.

'It is for a student who needs to understand the Holocaust.'

'How old is he?'

'*She* is fifteen.'

'Too young!'

'But not too young for Auschwitz,' said Mrs Pauli's husband.

Their friend considered. 'No,' he said at last. 'Not too young for Auschwitz. But tell her it is an evil book.'

'I wouldn't be lending it to her if I didn't think she already knows that,' said Gillian Pauli.

Gillian also taught me that writing is for those you write for, not for yourself, and that a book has power for both good and evil, and that power lasts long after those who wrote it have gone.

Years later, I would read psychiatric research showing that just one violent teenager may turn another fifteen violent or vicious, and they too will spread the disease. But by then I knew kindness can be contagious too.

It sounds simple, doesn't it? Too simple. Be kind, especially to those who are troubled and lash out, and that kindness will spread. Be compassionate, and that compassion will travel to others too. But while some of the underlying truths of the universe may be too complex to understand, this one is not: whatever you do that is evil or kind or compassionate will multiply, even if you never know how far it spreads.

At last I began to plot out this book. But first I requested permission to speak to the Holocaust survivors who volunteered at the museum. I asked them the question I had already asked many of those who had returned from the Japanese prison camps of World War II: 'How did you survive?'

I expected they would give the same answer I had heard from prison camp survivors: 'If you had a mate, you'd have a better chance to get back home. When you were ill or in despair, your mate would help you, and you would help them.'

I expected the museum volunteers to tell me that those who had a gift for friendship were more likely to live.

They said instead it was mostly a matter of luck. You might be allowed to live. You might be placed where everyone died, though in their stories there were times when their courage, intelligence and endurance might have meant they lived when others died.

Nor did those extraordinary volunteers say they had a greater capacity for friendship. Instead each said that after the war they hated; and that each, slowly, had learned to love again.

In the words of one man: 'The day they put my son into my arms I saw that my heart was so filled with hate there was little room to love my son. I knew I must become a man of love, not a man of hate, for my son.'

All said it was not easy to forgive. Some said that every day they had to forgive once again, put aside hate and take up love.

Forgiveness can be the hardest thing in the world. But it must be done, for your own sake, as well as for your family and the world, even if it must be done again every day of life.

You must forgive.

For years I thought I could not forgive the terrors of the past. Now that I have been taught, by those people who return love to a world that gave them so much hate, that forgiveness may need to be redone time and again, I know that you haven't failed if you find you must forgive over and over again. But if you don't forgive, the ogres — those who have hurt you — have won, because the fear and hatred they bred is part of you.

The crafting of this book is, in large part, a gift from Lisa Berryman, whose insistence on publishing only the best of what

I am capable of with every book has made me a far deeper writer than I could have imagined. In a world where publishing so often focuses on the facile, the genre that sold best last year, Cristina Cappelluto and James Kellow of HarperCollins have created a team that produces not just their bestsellers, but works they believe are important. When writing this book I never once had to think, 'Will HarperCollins reject this because it might not sell?'

Both Cristina and James also fight for the existence of the Australian book industry, currently under threat from government and Productivity Commission 'reforms' that might drive us back to the days of only decades ago when Australian writers could only survive by publishing and even living overseas while writing books for international audiences, not ones that spoke specifically to the people of this land.

It is perhaps not a coincidence that my character Johannes was sent to a camp that was first established to imprison, silence and eventually kill Polish writers and intellectuals who spoke out against Hitler. You do not have to kill writers to silence them these days, or even burn their books. All you need to do is destroy the industry that publishes them.

To the two Kates, Kate Burnitt and Kate O'Donnell, once again more thanks than I can say, and to Angela Marshall, who, as always, takes dyslexic gibberish and returns a readable manuscript, matched with an encyclopaedic knowledge of history and natural history that does not match my own, so that we each contribute to a decades-long dialogue and friendship. This book is hers as well.

It also belongs to Father Peter Day, who, when I was faced with tragedy while writing this book, showed me that loss must always be the other face of love, and love the other face of loss.

'Hold loss gently,' he told me. 'Hold it out in front of you, so you can see around it, and see the beauty and love in the world too.' Without Peter, I could not have continued writing this book.

Those who identified themselves as Christians during the Holocaust behaved in many ways. Some came to a convenient agreement with fascist authorities. Others looked away. Some fought evil in small ways, or large. And many died, in concentration camps and elsewhere, because they acted upon one of the inexorable tenets of Christianity: 'love thy neighbour as thyself'.

This book also is about some of those, as well as people like Johannes's family, and Georg's, who were sent to concentration camps not for being Jewish, or even for opposing fascism, but simply because their labour was needed.

It is important to remember that using race or religion as a scapegoat for our secret fears or anguish is evil. But it is also important to remember that the worst evils of the Holocaust could only happen once the fascists had removed most of those who had the insight and the courage to speak out against them.

As a quote attributed to philosopher Edmund Burke states, 'The only thing necessary for the triumph of evil is for good men to do nothing.'

We *can* change the world. I've seen it happen in my lifetime. People of goodwill work till change comes slowly — change for good is never as fast as you would like.

As Johannes says in this book, my tools are words. Yours will be different. He also acknowledges it is not easy to slay ogres either. But I do believe this: if you stand up for what is right, in small things or in large, slowly others will stand beside you … and then others too. Perhaps all change for good begins with one person.

Perhaps that person will be you.

Jackie French AM is an award-winning writer, wombat negotiator, the 2014–2015 Australian Children's Laureate and the 2015 Senior Australian of the Year. She is regarded as one of Australia's most popular children's authors and writes across all genres — from picture books, history, fantasy, ecology and sci-fi to her much loved historical fiction. 'Share a Story' was the primary philosophy behind Jackie's two-year term as Laureate.

jackiefrench.com
facebook.com/authorjackiefrench